THE CITY OF EMBER

Jeanne DuPrau

CORGI BOOKS

THE CITY OF EMBER
A CORGI BOOK 978 0 552 55998 0

First published in the US by Random House Children's Books,
a division of Random House Inc., New York

First published in Great Britain by Doubleday,
an imprint of Random House Children's Books
A Random House Group Company

Doubleday edition published 2004
First Corgi edition published 2005
This tie-in edition published 2008

1 3 5 7 9 10 8 6 4 2

Copyright © Jeanne DuPrau, 2004
Map by Chris Riely

 cityofember.com

The Random House Group Limited supports the Forest Stewardship Council (FSC), the
leading international forest certification organization. All our titles that are printed on
Greenpeace-approved FSC-certified paper carry the FSC logo. Our paper procurement policy
can be found at www.rbooks.co.uk/environment.

Corgi Books are published by Random House Children's Books,
61–63 Uxbridge Road, London W5 5SA

www.kidsatrandomhouse.co.uk
www.rbooks.co.uk

Addresses for companies within The Random House Group Limited can be found at:
www.randomhouse.co.uk/offices.htm

THE RANDOM HOUSE GROUP Limited Reg. No. 954009

A CIP catalogue record for this book is available from the British Library.

Printed in the UK by CPI Bookmarque, Croydon, CR0 4TD.

Contents

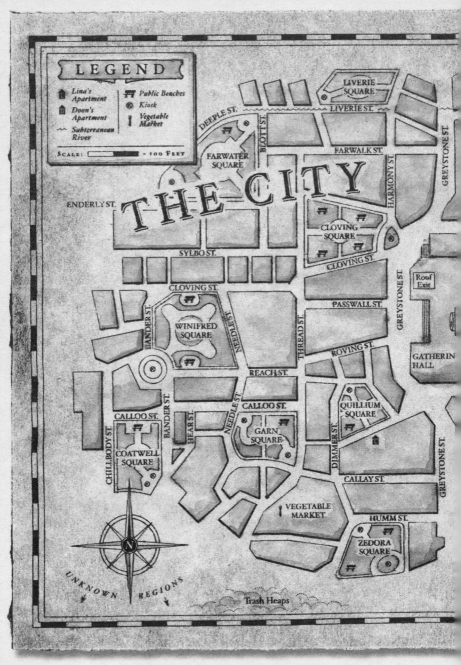

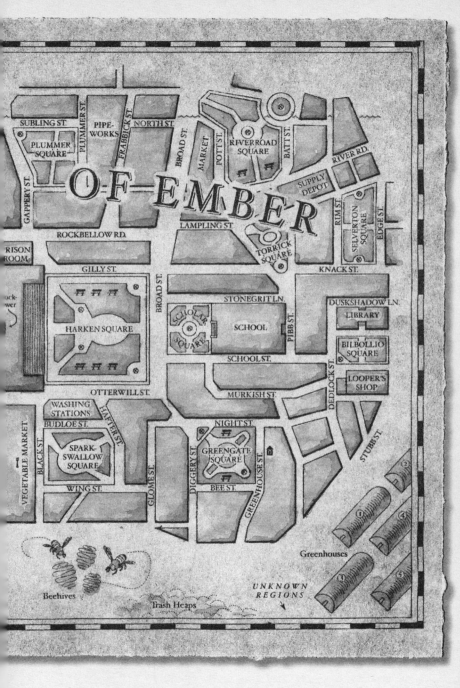

THE CITY OF
EMBER

The Instructions

When the city of Ember was just built and not yet inhabited, the chief builder and the assistant builder, both of them weary, sat down to speak of the future.

'They must not leave the city for at least two hundred years,' said the chief builder. 'Or perhaps two hundred and twenty.'

'Is that long enough?' asked his assistant.

'It should be. We can't know for sure.'

'And when the time comes,' said the assistant, 'how will they know what to do?'

'We'll provide them with instructions, of course,' the chief builder replied.

'But who will keep the instructions? Who can we trust to keep them safe and secret all that time?'

'The mayor of the city will keep the instructions,' said the chief builder. 'We'll put them in a box with a timed lock, set to open on the proper date.'

'And will we tell the mayor what's in the box?'

the assistant asked.

'No, just that it's information they won't need and must not see until the box opens of its own accord.'

'So the first mayor will pass the box to the next mayor, and that one to the next, and so on down through the years, all of them keeping it secret, all that time?'

'What else can we do?' asked the chief builder. 'Nothing about this endeavour is certain. There may be no one left in the city by then or no safe place for them to come back to.'

So the first mayor of Ember was given the box, told to guard it carefully, and solemnly sworn to secrecy. When she grew old, and her time as mayor was up, she explained about the box to her successor, who also kept the secret carefully, as did the next mayor. Things went as planned for many years. But the seventh mayor of Ember was less honourable than the ones who'd come before him, and more desperate. He was ill – he had the coughing sickness that was common in the city then – and he thought the box might hold a secret that would save his life. He took it from its hiding place in the basement of the Gathering Hall and brought it home with him, where he attacked it with a hammer.

But his strength was failing by then. All he man-aged to do was dent the lid a little. And before he could return the box to its official hiding place or tell his successor about it, he died. The box ended up at the back of a closet, shoved behind some old bags and bundles. There it sat, unnoticed, year after year, until its time arrived, and the lock quietly clicked open.

CHAPTER 1

Assignment Day

In the city of Ember, the sky was always dark. The only light came from great flood lamps mounted on the buildings and at the tops of poles in the middle of the larger squares. When the lights were on, they cast a yellowish glow over the streets; people walking by threw long shadows that shortened and then stretched out again. When the lights were off, as they were between nine at night and six in the morning, the city was so dark that people might as well have been wearing blindfolds.

Sometimes darkness fell in the middle of the day. The city of Ember was old, and everything in it, including the power lines, was in need of repair. So now and then the lights would flicker and go out. These were terrible moments for the people of Ember. As they came to a halt in the middle of the street or stood stock-still in their houses, afraid to move in the utter blackness, they were reminded of something they preferred not to think about: that some day the lights of the city might go out and never come back on.

But most of the time life proceeded as it always had. Grown people did their work, and younger people, until they reached the age of twelve, went to school. On the last day of their final year, which was called Assignment Day, they were given jobs to do.

The graduating students occupied Room Eight of the Ember School. On Assignment Day of the year 241, this classroom, usually noisy first thing in the morning, was completely silent. All twenty-four students sat upright and still at the desks they had grown too big for. They were waiting.

The desks were arranged in four rows of six, one behind the other. In the last row sat a slender girl named Lina Mayfleet. She was winding a strand of her long, dark hair around her finger, winding and unwinding it again and again. Sometimes she plucked at a thread on her ragged cape or bent over to pull on her socks, which were loose and tended to slide down around her ankles. One of her feet tapped the floor softly.

In the second row was a boy named Doon Harrow. He sat with his shoulders hunched, his eyes squeezed shut in concentration and his hands clasped tightly together. His hair looked rumpled, as if he hadn't combed it for a while. He had dark, thick eyebrows, which made him look serious at the best of times and, when he was anxious or angry, came together to form a straight line across his forehead. His brown corduroy jacket was so old that its ridges had flattened out.

Both the girl and the boy were making urgent wishes. Doon's wish was very specific. He repeated it over and over again, his lips moving slightly, as if he could make it come true by saying it a thousand times. Lina was making her wish in pictures rather than in words. In her mind's eye, she saw herself running through the streets of the city in a red jacket. She made this picture as bright and real as she could.

Lina looked up and gazed around the schoolroom. She said a silent goodbye to everything that had been familiar for so long. Goodbye to the map of the city of Ember in its scarred wooden frame and the cabinet whose shelves held *The Book of Numbers, The Book of Letters,* and *The Book of the City of Ember.* Goodbye to the cabinet drawers labelled 'New Paper' and 'Old Paper'. Goodbye to the three electric lights in the ceiling that seemed always, no matter where you sat, to cast the shadow of your head over the page you were writing on. And goodbye to their teacher, Miss Thorn, who had finished her Last Day of School speech, wishing them luck in the lives they were about to begin. Now, having run out of things to say, she was standing at her desk with her frayed shawl clasped around her shoulders. And still the mayor, the guest of honour, had not arrived.

Someone's foot scraped back and forth on the floor. Miss Thorn sighed. Then the door rattled open, and the mayor walked in. He looked annoyed, as though *they* were the ones who were late.

'Welcome, Mayor Cole,' said Miss Thorn. She held out her hand to him.

The mayor made his mouth into a smile. 'Miss Thorn,' he said, enfolding her hand. 'Greetings. Another year.' The mayor was a vast, heavy man, so big in the middle that his arms looked small and dangling. In one hand he held a little cloth bag.

He lumbered to the front of the room and faced the students. His grey, drooping face appeared to be made of something stiffer than ordinary skin; it rarely moved except for making the smile that was on it now.

'Young people of the Highest Class,' the mayor began. He stopped and scanned the room for several moments; his eyes seemed to look out from far back inside his head. He nodded slowly. 'Assignment Day now, isn't it? Yes. First we get our education. Then we serve our city.' Again his eyes moved back and forth along the rows of students, and again he nodded, as if someone had confirmed what he'd said. He put the little bag on Miss Thorn's desk and rested his hand on it. 'What will that service be, eh? Perhaps you're wondering.' He did his smile again, and his heavy cheeks folded like drapes.

Lina's hands were cold. She wrapped her cape around her and pressed her hands between her knees. Please hurry, Mr Mayor, she said silently. Please just let us choose and get it over with. Doon, in his mind, was saying the same thing, only he didn't say please.

'Something to remember,' the mayor said, holding up one finger. 'Job you draw today is for three years. Then, Evaluation. Are you good at your job? Fine. You may keep it. Are you unsatisfactory? Is there a greater need elsewhere? You will be re-assigned. It is *extremely important*,' he said, jabbing his finger at the class, 'for all . . . work . . . of Ember . . . to be done. To be *properly* done.'

He picked up the bag and pulled open the drawstring. 'So. Let us begin. Simple procedure. Come up one at a time. Reach into this bag. Take one slip of paper. Read it out loud.' He smiled and nodded. The flesh under his chin bulged in and out. 'Who cares to be first?'

No one moved. Lina stared down at the top of her desk. There was a long silence. Then Lizzie Bisco, one of Lina's best friends, sprang to her feet. 'I would like to be first,' she said in her breathless high voice.

'Good. Walk forward.'

Lizzie went to stand by the mayor. Because of her orange hair, she looked like a bright spark next to him.

'Now choose.' The mayor held out the bag with one hand and put the other behind his back, as if to show he would not interfere.

Lizzie reached into the bag and withdrew a tightly folded square of paper. She unfolded it carefully. Lina couldn't see the look on Lizzie's face, but she could hear the disappointment in her voice as she read out loud: 'Supply Depot clerk.'

'Very good,' said the mayor. 'A vital job.'

Lizzie trudged back to her desk. Lina smiled at her, but Lizzie made a sour face. Supply Depot clerk wasn't a bad job, but it was a dull one. The Supply Depot clerks sat behind a long counter, took orders from the storekeepers of Ember, and sent the carriers down to bring up what was wanted from the vast network of storerooms beneath Ember's streets. The storerooms held supplies of every kind – canned food, clothes, furniture, blankets, light bulbs, medicine, pots and pans, reams of paper, soap, more light bulbs – everything the people of Ember could possibly need. The clerks sat at their ledger books all day, recording the orders that came in and the goods that went out. Lizzie didn't like to sit still; she would have been better suited to something else, Lina thought – messenger, maybe, the job Lina wanted for herself. Messengers ran through the city all day, going everywhere, seeing everything.

'Next,' said the mayor.

This time two people stood up at once, Orly Gordon and Chet Noam. Orly quickly sat down again, and Chet approached the mayor.

'Choose, young man,' the mayor said.

Chet chose. He unfolded his scrap of paper. 'Electrician's helper,' he read, and his wide face broke into a smile. Lina heard someone take a quick breath. She looked over to see Doon pressing a hand against his mouth.

You never knew, each year, exactly which jobs would be offered. Some years there were several good jobs, like greenhouse helper, timekeeper's assistant, or messenger, and no bad jobs at all. Other years, jobs like Pipeworks labourer, trash sifter and mould scraper were mixed in. But there would always be at least one or two jobs for electrician's helper. Fixing the electricity was the most important job in Ember, and more people worked at it than at anything else.

Orly Gordon was next. She got the job of building repair assistant, which was a good job for Orly. She was a strong girl and liked hard work. Vindie Chance was made a greenhouse helper. She gave Lina a big grin as she went back to her seat. She'll get to work with Clary, Lina thought. Lucky. So far no one had picked a really bad job. Perhaps this time there would be no bad jobs at all.

The idea gave her courage. Besides, she had reached the point where the suspense was giving her a stomach ache. So as Vindie sat down – even before the mayor could say 'Next' – she stood up and stepped forward.

The little bag was made of faded green material, gathered at the top with a black string. Lina hesitated a moment, then put her hand inside and fingered the bits of paper. Feeling as if she were stepping off a high building, she picked one.

She unfolded it. The words were written in black ink, in small careful printing. PIPEWORKS LABOURER, they said. She stared at them.

'Out loud, please,' the mayor said.

'Pipeworks labourer,' Lina said in a choked whisper.

'Louder,' said the mayor.

'Pipeworks labourer,' Lina said again, her voice loud and cracked. There was a sigh of sympathy from the class. Keeping her eyes on the floor, Lina went back to her desk and sat down.

Pipeworks labourers worked below the store-rooms in the deep labyrinth of tunnels that contained Ember's water and sewer pipes. They spent their days stopping up leaks and replacing pipe joints. It was wet, cold work; it could even be dangerous. A swift underground river ran through the Pipeworks, and every now and then someone fell into it and was lost. People were lost occasionally in the tunnels, too, if they strayed too far.

Lina stared miserably down at a letter B someone had scratched into her desktop long ago. Almost anything would have been better than Pipeworks labourer. Greenhouse helper had been her second choice. She imagined with longing the warm air and earthy smell of the greenhouse, where she could have worked with Clary, the greenhouse manager, someone she'd known all her life. She would have been content as a doctor's assistant, too, binding up cuts and bones. Even street-sweeper or cart-puller would have been better. At least then she could have stayed above ground, with space and people around her. She thought going down into the Pipeworks must be like being buried alive.

One by one, the other students chose their jobs. None of them got such a wretched job as hers. Finally the last person rose from his chair and walked forward.

It was Doon. His dark eyebrows were drawn together in a frown of concentration. His hands, Lina saw, were clenched into fists at his sides.

Doon reached into the bag and took out the last scrap of paper. He paused a minute, pressing it tightly in his hand.

'Go on,' said the mayor. 'Read.'

Unfolding the paper, Doon read: 'Messenger.' He scowled, crumpled the paper and dashed it to the floor.

Lina gasped; the whole class rustled in surprise. Why would anyone be angry to get the job of messenger?

'Bad behaviour!' cried the mayor. His eyes bulged and his face darkened. 'Go to your seat immediately.'

Doon kicked the crumpled paper into a corner. Then he stalked back to his desk and flung himself down.

The mayor took a short breath and blinked furiously. 'Disgraceful,' he said, glaring at Doon. 'A childish display of temper! Students should be *glad* to work for their city. Ember will prosper if all citizens ... do ... their ... best.' He held up a stern finger as he said this and moved his eyes slowly from one face to the next.

Suddenly Doon spoke up. 'But Ember is *not* prospering!' he cried. 'Everything is getting worse and worse!'

'Silence!' cried the mayor.

'The blackouts!' cried Doon. He jumped from his seat. 'The lights go out all the time now! And the shortages, there's shortages of everything! If no one does anything about it, something terrible is going to happen!'

Lina listened with a pounding heart. What was wrong with Doon? Why was he so upset? He was taking things too seriously, as he always did.

Miss Thorn strode to Doon and put a hand on his shoulder. 'Sit down now,' she said quietly. But

Doon remained standing.

The mayor glared. For a few moments he said nothing. Then he smiled, showing a neat row of grey teeth. 'Miss Thorn,' he said. 'Who might this young man be?'

'I am Doon Harrow,' said Doon.

'I will remember you,' said the mayor. He gave Doon a long look, then turned to the class and smiled his smile again.

'Congratulations to all,' he said. 'Welcome to Ember's work force. Miss Thorn. Class. Thank you.'

The mayor shook hands with Miss Thorn and departed. The students gathered their coats and caps and filed out of the classroom. Lina walked down the Wide Hallway with Lizzie, who said, 'Poor you! I thought *I* picked a bad one, but you got the worst. I feel lucky compared to you.' Once they were out the door, Lizzie said goodbye and scurried away, as if Lina's bad luck were a disease she might catch.

Lina stood on the steps for a moment and gazed across Harken Square, where people walked briskly, bundled up cosily in their coats and scarves, or talked to one another in the pools of light beneath the great streetlamps. A boy in a red messenger's jacket ran toward the Gathering Hall. On Otterwill Street, a man pulled a cart filled with sacks of potatoes. And in the buildings all around the square, rows of lighted windows shone bright yellow and deep gold.

Lina sighed. *This* was where she wanted to be, up here where everything happened, not down underground.

Someone tapped her on the shoulder. Startled, she turned and saw Doon behind her. His thin face looked pale. 'Will you trade with me?' he asked.

'Trade?'

'Trade jobs. I don't want to waste my time being a messenger. I want to help save the city, not run around carrying gossip.'

Lina gaped at him. 'You'd rather be in the *Pipeworks*?'

'Electrician's helper is what I wanted,' Doon said. 'But Chet won't trade, of course. Pipeworks is second best.'

'But why?'

'Because the generator is in the Pipeworks,' said Doon.

Lina knew about the generator, of course. In some mysterious way, it turned the running of the river into power for the city. You could feel its deep rumble when you stood in Plummer Square.

'I need to see the generator,' Doon said. 'I have . . . I have ideas about it.' He thrust his hands into his pockets. 'So,' he said, 'will you trade?'

'Yes!' cried Lina. 'Messenger is the job I want most!' And not a useless job at all, in her opinion. People couldn't be expected to trudge halfway across the city every time they wanted to communicate with someone. Messengers connected everyone to everyone else. Anyway, whether it was important or not, the job of messenger just happened to be perfect for Lina. She loved to run. She could run for ever. And she loved exploring every nook and cranny of the city, which was what a messenger got to do.

'All right then,' said Doon. He handed her his crumpled piece of paper, which he must have retrieved from the floor. Lina reached into her pocket, pulled out her slip of paper and handed it to him.

'Thank you,' he said.

'You're welcome,' said Lina. Happiness sprang up in her, and happiness always made her want to run. She took the steps three at a time and sped down Broad Street towards home.

CHAPTER 2

A Message to the Mayor

Lina often took different routes between school and home. Sometimes, just for variety, she'd go all the way around Sparkswallow Square, or way up by the shoe repair shops on Liverie Street. But today she took the shortest route because she was eager to get home and tell her news.

She ran fast and easily through the streets of Ember. Every corner, every alley, every building was familiar to her. She always knew where she was, though most streets looked more or less the same. All of them were lined with old two-storey stone buildings, the wood of their window frames and doors long unpainted. On the street level were shops; above the shops were the apartments where people lived. Every building, at the place where the wall met the roof, was equipped with a row of floodlights – big cone-shaped lamps that cast a strong yellow glare.

Stone walls, lighted windows, lumpy, muffled

shapes of people – Lina flew by them. Her slender legs felt immensely strong, like the wood of a bow that flexes and springs. She darted around obstacles – broken furniture left for the trash heaps or for scavengers, stoves and refrigerators that were past repair, pedlars sitting on the pavement with their wares spread out around them. She leaped over cracks and potholes.

When she came to Hafter Street, she slowed a little. This street was deep in shadow. Four of its streetlamps were out and had not been fixed. For a second, Lina thought of the rumour she'd heard about light bulbs: that some kinds were completely gone. She was used to shortages of things – everyone was – but not of light bulbs! If the bulbs for the streetlamps ran out, the only lights would be inside the buildings. What would happen then? How could people find their way through the streets in the dark?

Somewhere inside her, a black worm of dread stirred. She thought about Doon's outburst in class. Could things really be as bad as he said? She didn't want to believe it. She pushed the thought away.

As she turned onto Budloe Street, she sped up again. She passed a line of customers waiting to get into the vegetable market, their shopping bags draped over their arms. At the corner of Oliver Street, she dodged a group of washers trudging along with bags of laundry, and some movers carrying away a broken table. She passed a street-sweeper shoving dust around with his broom. I am so lucky, she thought, to have the job I want. And because of Doon Harrow, of all people.

When they were younger, Lina and Doon had been friends. Together they had explored the back alleys and dimly lit edges of the city. But in their fourth year of school, they had begun to grow apart. It started one day during the hour of free time, when the children in their class were playing on the front steps of the school. 'I can go down three steps at a time,' someone would boast. 'I can hop down on one foot!' someone else would say. The others would chime in, 'I can do a handstand against the pillar!' 'I can leapfrog over the trash can!' As soon as one child did something, all the rest would do it, too, to prove they could.

Lina could do it all, even when the dares got wilder. She yelled out the wildest one of all: 'I can climb the light pole!' For a second everyone just stared at her. But Lina dashed across the street, took off her shoes and socks, and wrapped herself around the cold metal of the pole. Pushing with her bare feet, she inched upward. She didn't get very far before she lost her grip and fell back down. The children laughed, and so did she. 'I didn't say I'd climb to the top,' she explained. 'I just said I'd climb it.'

The others swarmed forward to try. Lizzie wouldn't take off her socks – her feet were too cold, she said – so she kept sliding back. Fordy Penn wasn't strong enough to get more than a foot off the ground. Next came Doon. He took his shoes and socks off and placed them neatly at the foot of the pole. Then he announced, in his serious way, 'I'm going to the top.' He clasped the pole and started upwards, pushing with his feet, his knees sticking out to the sides. He pulled himself upwards, pushed again – he was higher now than Lina had been – but suddenly his hands slid and he came plummeting down. He landed on his bottom with his legs poking up in the air. Lina laughed. She shouldn't have; he might have been hurt. But he looked so funny that she couldn't help it.

He wasn't hurt. He could have jumped up, grinned and walked away. But Doon didn't take things lightly. When he heard Lina and the others laughing, his face darkened. His temper rose in him like hot water. 'Don't you dare laugh at me,' he said to Lina. 'I did better than you did! That was a stupid idea anyway, a stupid, stupid idea to climb that pole. . .' And as he was shouting, red in the face, their teacher, Mrs Polster, came out onto the steps and saw him. She took him by the shirt collar to the school director's office, where he got a scolding he didn't think he deserved.

After that day, Lina and Doon barely looked at each other when they passed in the hallway. At first it was because they were fuming about what had happened. Doon didn't like being laughed at; Lina didn't like being shouted at. After a while the memory of the light-pole incident faded, but by then they had got out of the habit of friendship. By the time they were twelve, they knew each other only as classmates. Lina was friends with Vindie Chance, Orly Gordon and, most of all, red-haired Lizzie Bisco, who could run almost as fast as Lina and could talk three times faster.

Now, as Lina sped towards home, she felt immensely grateful to Doon and hoped he'd come to no harm in the Pipeworks. Maybe they'd be friends again. She'd like to ask him about the Pipeworks. She was curious about it.

When she got to Greystone Street, she passed Clary Laine, who was probably on her way to the greenhouses. Clary waved to her and called out, 'What job?' and Lina called back, 'Messenger!' and ran on.

Lina lived in Quillium Square, over the yarn shop run by her grandmother. When she got to the shop, she burst in the door and cried, 'Granny! I'm a messenger!'

Granny's shop had once been a tidy place, where each ball of yarn and spool of thread had its spot in the cubbyholes that lined the walls. All the yarn and thread came from old clothes that had gotten too shabby to be worn. Granny unravelled sweaters and picked apart dresses and jackets and trousers; she wound the yarn into balls and the thread onto spools, and people bought them to use in making new clothes.

These days, the shop was a mess. Long loops and strands of yarn dangled out of the cubbyholes, and the browns and greys and purples were mixed in with the ochres and olive greens and dark blues. Granny's customers often had to spend half an hour unsnarling the rust-red yarn from the mud-brown, or trying to fish out the end of a thread from a tangled wad. Granny wasn't much help. Most days she just dozed behind the counter in her rocking chair.

That's where she was when Lina burst in with her news. Lina saw that Granny had forgotten to knot up her hair that morning – it was standing out from her head in a wild white frizz.

Granny stood up, looking puzzled. 'You aren't a messenger, dear, you're a schoolgirl,' she said.

'But Granny, today was Assignment Day. I got my job. And I'm a messenger!'

Granny's eyes lit up, and she slapped her hand down on the counter. 'I remember!' she cried. 'Messenger, that's a grand job! You'll be good at it.'

Lina's little sister toddled out from behind the counter on unsteady legs. She had a round face and round brown eyes. At the top of her head was a sprig of brown hair tied up with a scrap of red yarn. She grabbed onto Lina's knees. 'Wy-na, Wy-na!' she said.

Lina bent over and took the child's hands. 'Poppy! Your big sister got a good job! Are you happy, Poppy? Are you proud of me?'

Poppy said something that sounded like, 'Hoppyhoppyhoppy!' Lina laughed, hoisted her up and danced with her around the shop.

Lina loved her little sister so much that it was like an ache under her ribs. The baby and Granny were all the family she had now. Two years ago, when the coughing sickness was raging through the city again, her father had died. Some months later, her mother, giving birth to Poppy, had died, too. Lina missed her parents with an ache that was as strong as what she felt for Poppy, only it was a hollow feeling instead of a full one.

'When do you start?' asked Granny.

'Tomorrow,' said Lina. 'I report to the messengers' station at eight o'clock.'

'You'll be a famous messenger,' said Granny. 'Fast and famous.'

Taking Poppy with her, Lina went out of the shop and climbed the stairs to their apartment. It was a small apartment, only four rooms, but there was enough stuff in it to fill twenty. There were things that had belonged to Lina's parents, her grandparents and even *their* grandparents – old, broken, cracked, threadbare things that had been patched and repaired dozens or hundreds of times. People in Ember rarely threw anything away. They made the best possible use of what they had.

In Lina's apartment, layers of worn rugs and carpets covered the floor, making it soft but uneven underfoot. Against one wall squatted a sagging couch with round wooden balls for legs, and on the couch were blankets and pillows, so many that you had to toss some on the floor before you could sit down. Against the opposite wall stood two wobbly tables that held a clutter of plates and bottles, cups and bowls, unmatching forks and spoons, little piles of scrap paper, bits of string wound up in untidy wads, and a few stubby pencils. There were four lamps, two tall ones that stood on the floor and two short ones that stood on tables. And in uneven lines up near the ceiling were hooks that held coats and shawls and nightgowns and sweaters, shelves that held pots and pans, jars with unreadable labels and boxes of buttons and pins.

Where there were no shelves, the walls had been decorated with things of beauty – a label from a can of peaches, a few dried yellow squash flowers, a strip of faded but still pretty purple cloth. There were drawings, too. Lina had done the drawings out of her imagination. They showed a city that looked somewhat like Ember, except that its buildings were lighter and taller and had more windows.

One of the drawings had fallen to the floor. Lina retrieved it and pinned it back up. She stood for a minute and looked at the pictures. Over and over, she'd drawn the same city. Sometimes she drew it as seen from afar, sometimes she chose one of its buildings and drew it in detail. She put in stairways and streetlamps and carts. Sometimes she tried to draw the people who lived in the city, though she wasn't good at drawing people – their heads always came out too small, and their hands looked like spiders. One picture showed a scene in which the people of the city greeted her when she arrived – the first person they had ever seen to come from elsewhere. They argued with each other about who should be the first to invite her home.

Lina could see this city so clearly in her mind she almost believed it was real. She knew it couldn't be, though. *The Book of the City of Ember,* which all children studied in school, taught otherwise. 'The city of Ember was made for us long ago by the Builders,' the book said. 'It is the only light in the dark world. Beyond Ember, the darkness goes on for ever in all directions.'

Lina had been to the outer border of Ember. She had stood at the edge of the trash heaps and gazed into the darkness beyond the city – the Unknown Regions. No one had ever gone far into the Unknown

Regions – or at least no one had gone far and returned. And no one had ever arrived in Ember from the Unknown Regions, either. As far as anyone knew, the darkness *did* go on for ever. Still, Lina wanted the other city to exist. In her imagination, it was so beautiful, and it seemed so real. Sometimes she longed to go there and take everyone in Ember with her.

But she wasn't thinking about the other city now. Today she was happy to be right where she was. She set Poppy on the couch. 'Wait there,' she said. She went into the kitchen, where there was an electric stove and a refrigerator that no longer worked and was used to store glasses and dishes so Poppy couldn't get at them. Above the refrigerator were shelves holding more pots and jars, more spoons and knives, a wind-up clock that Granny always forgot to wind, and a long row of cans. Lina tried to keep the cans in alphabetical order so she could find what she wanted quickly, but Granny always messed them up. Now, she saw, there were beans at the end of the row and tomatoes at the beginning. She picked out a can labelled BABY DRINK and a jar of boiled carrots, opened them, poured the liquid into a cup and the carrots into a little dish, and took these back to the baby on the couch.

Poppy dribbled Baby Drink down her chin. She ate some of her carrots and poked others between the couch cushions. For the moment, Lina felt almost perfectly happy. There was no need to think about the fate of the city right now. Tomorrow, she'd be a messenger! She wiped the orange goop off Poppy's chin. 'Don't worry,' she said. 'Everything will be all right.'

The messengers' headquarters was on Cloving Street, not far from the back of the Gathering Hall. When Lina arrived the next morning, she was greeted by Messenger Captain Allis Fleery, a bony woman with pale eyes and hair the colour of dust. 'Our new girl,' said Captain Fleery to the other messengers, a cluster of nine people who smiled and nodded at Lina. 'I have your jacket right here,' said the captain. She handed Lina a red jacket like the one all messengers wore. It was only a little too large.

From the clock tower of the Gathering Hall came a deep reverberating bong. 'Eight o'clock!' cried Captain Fleery. She waved a long arm. 'Take your stations!' As the clock sounded seven more times, the messengers scattered in all directions. The captain turned to Lina. 'Your station,' she said, 'is Garn Square.'

Lina nodded and started off, but the captain caught her by the collar. 'I haven't told you the rules,' she said. She held up a knobby finger. 'One: When a customer gives you a message, repeat it back to make sure you have it right. Two: Always wear your red jacket so people can identify you. Three: Go as fast as possible. Your customers pay twenty cents for every message, no matter how far you have to take it.'

Lina nodded. 'I always go fast,' she said.

'Four,' the captain went on. 'Deliver a message only to the person it's meant for, no one else.'

Lina nodded again. She bounced a little on her toes, eager to get going.

Captain Fleery smiled. 'Go,' she said, and Lina was off.

She felt strong and speedy and surefooted. She glanced at her reflection as she ran past the window of a furniture repair shop. She liked the look of her long dark hair flying out behind her, her long legs in their black socks and her flapping red jacket. Her face, which had never seemed especially remarkable, looked almost beautiful, because she looked so happy.

As soon as she came into Garn Square, a voice cried, 'Messenger!' Her first customer! It was old Natty Prine, calling to her from the bench where he always sat. 'This goes to Ravenet Parsons, eighteen Selverton Square,' he said. 'Bend down.'

She bent down so that her ear was close to his whiskery mouth.

The old man said in a slow, hoarse voice, 'My stove is broke, don't come for dinner. Repeat.'

Lina repeated the message.

'Good,' said Natty Prine. He gave Lina twenty cents, and she ran across the city to Selverton Square. There she found Ravenet Parsons also sitting on a bench. She recited the message to him.

'Old turniphead,' he growled. 'Lazy old fleaface. He just doesn't feel like cooking. No reply.'

Lina ran back to Garn Square, passing a group of Believers on the way. They were standing in a circle, holding hands, singing one of their cheerful songs. It seemed to Lina there were more Believers than ever these days. What they believed in she didn't know, but it must make them happy – they were always smiling.

Her next customer turned out to be Mrs Polster, the teacher of the fourth-year class. In Mrs Polster's class, they memorized passages from *The Book of the City of Ember* every week. Mrs Polster had charts on the walls for everything, with everyone's name listed. If you did something right, she made a green dot by your name. If you did something wrong, she made a red dot. 'What you need to learn, children,' she always said, in her resonant, precise voice, ' is the difference between right and wrong in every area of life. And once you learn the difference—' Here she would stop and point to the class, and the class would finish the sentence: 'You must always choose the right.' In every situation, Mrs Polster knew what the right choice was.

Now here was Mrs Polster again, looming over Lina and pronouncing her message. 'To Annisette Lafrond, thirty-nine Humm Street, as follows,' she said. 'My confidence in you has been seriously diminished since I heard about the disreputable activities in which you engaged on Thursday last. Please repeat.'

It took Lina three tries to get this right. 'Uh-oh, a red dot for me,' she said. Mrs Polster did not seem to find this amusing.

Lina had nineteen customers that first morning. Some of them had ordinary messages: 'I can't come on Tuesday.' 'Buy a pound of potatoes on your way home.' 'Please come and fix my front door.' Others had messages that made no sense to her at all, like Mrs Polster's. But it didn't matter. The wonderful part about being a messenger was not the messages but the places she got to go. She could go into the houses of people she didn't know and hidden alleyways and little rooms in the backs of stores. In just a few hours, she discovered all kinds of strange and interesting things.

For instance: Mrs Sample, the mender, had to sleep on her couch because her entire bedroom, almost up to the ceiling, was crammed with clothes to be mended. Dr Felinia Tower had the skeleton of a person hanging against her living-room wall, its bones all held in place with black strings. 'I study it,' she said when she saw Lina staring. 'I have to know how people are put together.' At a house on Calloo Street, Lina delivered a message to a worried-looking man whose living room was completely dark. 'I'm saving on light bulbs,' the man said. And when Lina took a message to the Can Café, she learned that on certain days the back room was used as a meeting place for people who liked to converse about Great Subjects. 'Do you think an Invisible Being is watching over us all the time?' she heard someone ask. 'Perhaps,' answered someone else. There was a long silence. 'And then again, perhaps not.'

All of it was interesting. She loved finding things out, and she loved running. And even by the end of the day, she wasn't tired. Running made her feel strong and big-hearted, it made her love the places she ran through and the people whose messages she delivered. She wished she could bring all of them the good news they so desperately wanted to hear.

Late in the afternoon, a young man came up to her, walking with a sort of sideways lurch. He was an odd-looking person – he had a very long neck with a bump in the middle and teeth so big they looked as if they were trying to escape from his mouth. His black, bushy hair stuck out from his head in untidy tufts. 'I have a message for the mayor, at the Gathering Hall,' he said. He paused to let the importance of this be understood. 'The mayor,' he said. 'Did you get that?'

'I got it,' said Lina.

'All right. Listen carefully. Tell him: Delivery at eight. From Looper. Repeat it back.'

'Delivery at eight. From Looper,' Lina repeated. It was an easy message.

'All right. No answer required.' He handed her twenty cents, and she sprinted away.

The Gathering Hall occupied one entire side of Harken Square, which was the city's central plaza. The square was paved with stone. It had a few benches bolted to the ground here and there, as well as a couple of kiosks for notices. Wide steps led up to the Gathering Hall, and fat columns framed its big door. The mayor's office was in the Gathering Hall. So were the offices of the clerks who kept track of which buildings had broken windows, what streetlamps needed repair, and the number of people in the city. There was the office of the timekeeper, who was in charge of the town clock. And there were offices for the guards who enforced the laws of Ember, now and then putting pickpockets or people who got in fights into the Prison Room, a small one-storey structure with a sloping roof that jutted out from one side of the building.

Lina ran up the steps and through the door into a broad hallway. On the left was a desk, and at the desk sat a guard: 'Barton Snode, Assistant Guard' said a badge on his chest. He was a big man, with wide shoulders, brawny arms and a thick neck. But his head looked as if it didn't belong to his body – it was small and round and topped with a fuzz of extremely short hair. His lower jaw jutted out and moved a little from side to side, as if he were chewing on something.

When he saw Lina, his jaw stopped moving for a moment and his lips curled upwards in a very small smile. 'Good day,' he said. 'What business brings you here today?'

'I have a message for the mayor.'

'Very good, very good.' Barton Snode heaved himself to his feet. 'Step this way.'

He led Lina down the corridor and opened a door marked 'Reception Room'.

'Wait here, please,' he said. 'The mayor is in his basement office on private business, but he will be up shortly.'

Lina went inside.

'I'll notify the mayor,' said Barton Snode. 'Please have a seat. The mayor will be right with you. Or pretty soon.' He left, closing the door behind him. A second later, the door opened again, and the guard's small fuzzy head reappeared. 'What *is* the message?' he asked.

'I have to give it to the mayor in person,' said Lina.

'Of course, of course,' said the guard. The door closed again. He doesn't seem very sure about things, Lina thought. Maybe he's new at his job.

The Reception Room was shabby, but Lina could tell that it had once been impressive. The walls were dark red, with brownish patches where the paint was peeling away. In the right-hand wall was a closed door. An ugly brown carpet lay on the floor, and on it stood a large armchair covered in itchy-looking red material, and several smaller chairs. A small table held a teapot and some cups, and a larger table in the middle of the room displayed a copy of *The Book of the City of Ember*, lying open as if someone were going to read from it. Portraits of all the mayors of the city since the beginning of time hung on the walls, staring solemnly from behind pieces of old window glass.

Lina sat in the big armchair and waited. No one came. She got up and wandered around the room. She bent over *The Book of the City of Ember* and read a few sentences: 'The citizens of Ember may not have luxuries, but the foresight of the Builders, who filled the storerooms at the beginning of time, has ensured that they will always have enough, and enough is all that a person of wisdom needs.'

She flipped a few pages. 'The Gathering Hall clock,' she read, 'measures the hours of night and day. It must never be allowed to run down. Without it, how would we know when to go to work and when to go to school? How would the light director know when to turn the lights on and when to turn them off again? It is the job of the timekeeper to wind the clock every week and to place the date sign in Harken Square every day. The timekeeper must perform these duties faithfully.'

Lina knew that not all timekeepers were as faithful as they should be. She'd heard of one, some years ago, who often forgot to change the date sign, so that it might say, 'Wednesday, Week 38, Year 227' for several days in a row. There had even been timekeepers who forgot to wind the clock, so that it might stand at noon or at midnight for hours at a time, causing a very long day or a very long night. The result was that no one really knew any more exactly what day of the week it was, or exactly how many years it had been since the building of the city – they called this the year 241, but it might have been 245 or 239 or 250. As long as the clock's deep boom rang out every hour, and the lights went on and off more or less regularly, it didn't seem to matter.

Lina left the book and examined the pictures of the mayors. The seventh mayor, Podd Morethwart, was her great-great – she didn't know how many greats – grandfather. He looked quite dreary, Lina thought. His cheeks were long and hollow, his mouth turned down at the corners, and there was a lost look in his eyes. The picture she liked best was of the fourth mayor, Jane Larket, who had a serene smile and fuzzy black hair.

Still no one came. She heard no sounds from the hallway. Maybe they'd forgotten her.

Lina went over to the closed door in the right-hand wall. She pulled it open and saw stairs going up. Maybe, while she waited, she'd just see where they went. She started upwards. At the top of the first flight was a closed door. Carefully, she opened it. She saw another hallway and more closed doors. She shut the door and kept going. Her footsteps sounded loud on the wood, and she was afraid someone would hear her and come and scold her. No doubt she was not supposed to be here. But no one came, and she climbed on, passing another closed door.

The Gathering Hall was the only building in Ember with three storeys. She had always wanted to stand on its roof and look out at the city. Maybe from there it would be possible to see beyond the city, into the Unknown Regions. If the bright city of her drawings really did exist, it would be out there somewhere.

At the top of the stairs, she came to a door marked 'Roof' and she pushed it open. Chilly air brushed against her skin. She was outside. Ahead of her was a flat gravel surface, and about ten paces away she could see the high wall of the clock tower.

She went to the edge of the roof. From there she could see the whole of Ember. Directly below was Harken Square, where people were moving this way and that, all of them appearing, from this top-down view, more round than tall. Beyond Harken Square, the lighted windows of the buildings made checkered lines, yellow and black, row after row, in all directions. She tried to see farther, across the Unknown Regions, but she couldn't. At the edges of the city, the lights were so far away that they made a kind of haze. She could see nothing beyond them but blackness.

She heard a shout from the square below. 'Look!' came a small but piercing voice. 'Someone on the roof!' She saw a few people stop and look up. 'Who is it? What's she doing up there?' someone cried. More people gathered, until a crowd was standing on the steps of the Gathering Hall. They see me! Lina thought, and it made her laugh. She waved at the crowd and did a few steps from the Bugfoot Scurry Dance, which she'd learned on Cloving Square Dance Day, and they laughed and shouted some more.

Then the door behind her burst open, and a huge guard with a bushy black beard was suddenly running towards her. 'Halt!' he shouted, though she wasn't going anywhere. He grabbed her by the arm. 'What are you doing here?'

'I was just curious,' said Lina, in her most inno-cent voice. 'I wanted to see the city from the roof.' She read the guard's name badge. It said, 'Redge Stabmark, Chief Guard'.

'Curiosity leads to trouble,' said Redge Stabmark. He peered down at the crowd. 'You have caused a commotion.' He pulled her towards the door and hustled her down all three flights of stairs. When they came out into the waiting room, Barton Snode was standing there looking flustered, his jaw twitching from side to side. Next to him was the mayor.

'A child causing trouble, Mayor Cole,' said the chief guard.

The mayor glared at her. 'I recall your face. From Assignment Day. Shame! Disgracing yourself in your new job.'

'I didn't mean to cause trouble,' said Lina. 'I was looking for you so I could deliver a message.'

'Shall we put her in the Prison Room for a day or two?' asked the chief guard.

The mayor frowned. He pondered a moment. 'What is the message?' he said. He bent down so that Lina could speak into his ear. She noticed that he smelled a little like overcooked turnips.

'Delivery at eight,' Lina whispered. 'From Looper.'

The mayor smiled a tight little smile. He turned to the guard. 'Just a child's antics,' he said. 'We will let it go this time. From now on,' he said to Lina, 'behave yourself.'

'Yes, Mr Mayor,' said Lina.

'And you,' said the mayor, turning to the assistant guard and shaking a thick finger at him, 'watch visitors much . . . more . . . carefully.'

Barton Snode blinked and nodded.

Lina ran for the door. Outside, the small crowd was still standing by the steps. A few of them cheered as Lina came out. Others frowned at her and muttered words like 'mischief' and 'silliness' and 'show-off'. Lina felt embarrassed suddenly. She hadn't meant to show off. She hurried past, out into Otterwill Street, and started to run.

She didn't see Doon, who was among those watching her. He had been on his way home from his first day in the Pipeworks when he'd come across the cluster of people gazing up at the roof of the Gathering Hall and laughing. He was tired and chilly. The bottoms of his trouser legs were wet, and mud clung to his shoes and smeared his hands. When he raised his eyes and saw the small figure next to the clock tower, he realized right away that it was Lina. He saw her raise her arm and wave and hop about, and for a second he wondered what it would be like to be up there, looking out over the whole city, laughing and waving. When Lina came down, he wanted to speak to her. But he knew he was filthy-looking and that she would ask him questions he didn't want to answer. So he turned away. Walking fast, he headed for home.

CHAPTER 3

Under Ember

That morning, Doon had arrived at the Pipeworks
full of anticipation. This was the world of serious
work at last, where he would get a chance to do something useful. What he'd learned in school, and from
his father, and from his own investigations – he could
put it all to good purpose now.

He pushed open the heavy Pipeworks door and
stepped inside. The air smelled strongly of dampness
and mouldy rubber, which seemed to him a pleasant,
interesting smell. He strode up a hallway where yellow
slickers hung from pegs on the walls. At the end of the
hallway was a room full of people, some of them
sitting on benches and pulling on knee-high rubber
boots, some struggling into their slickers, some buck-
ling on tool belts. A raucous clamour filled the room.
Doon watched from the doorway, eager to join in but
not sure what to do.

After a moment a man emerged from the throng.

He thrust out a hand. 'Lister Munk, Pipeworks director,' he said. 'You're the new boy, right? What size feet do you have – large, medium, or small?'

'Medium,' said Doon, and Lister found him a slicker and a pair of boots. The boots were so ancient that their green rubber was cracked all over, as if covered with spiderwebs. He gave Doon a tool belt, too, in which were wrenches and hammers, spools of wire and tape, and tubes of some sort of black goop.

'You'll be in Tunnel ninety-seven today,' Lister said. 'Arlin Froll will go down with you and show you what to do.' He pointed at a short, delicate-looking girl with a white-blonde braid down her back. 'She may not look like an expert, but she is.'

Doon buckled his tool belt around his waist and put on his slicker, which, for some reason, smelled like sweaty feet. 'This way,' said Arlin, without saying hello or smiling. She wove through the crowd of workers to a door marked 'Stairway' and opened it.

Stone steps led so far down that Doon couldn't see the end of them. On either side was a sheer wall of dark reddish stone, glistening with dampness. There was no railing. Along the ceiling ran a single wire from which a light bulb hung every few yards. Water stood in shallow pools on each stair, in the hollow worn into the stones by years of footsteps.

They started down. Doon concentrated on his feet – the clumsy boots made it hard not to stumble.

As they went deeper, he began to hear a low roar, so low he seemed to hear it more with his stomach than his ears. It grew louder and louder – was it a machine of some kind? Maybe the generator?

The stairway came to an end at a door marked 'Main Tunnel'. Arlin opened it, and as they stepped through, Doon realized that the sound he had been hearing wasn't a machine. It was the river.

He stood still, staring. Like most people, he had never been really sure what a river was – just that it was water that somehow flowed on its own. He'd imagined it would be like the clear, narrow stream that came out of the kitchen tap, only bigger, and horizontal instead of vertical. But this was something entirely different – not a stream of water, but endless tons of it pouring by. Wide as the widest street in Ember, churning and dipping and swirling, the river roared past, its turbulent surface like black, liquid glass scattered with flecks of light. Doon had never seen anything that moved so fast, and he had never heard such a thunderous, heart-stopping roar.

The path they stood on was about six feet wide and ran parallel to the river for farther than Doon could see in both directions. In the wall along the path were openings that must lead, Doon thought, to the tunnels that branched everywhere below the city. A string of lights like the one in the stairway hung high up against the arched ceiling.

Doon knew he was standing beneath the north edge of Ember. In school, you were taught to remember the directions this way: north was the direction of the river; south was the direction of the greenhouses; east was the direction of the school; and west was the direction left over, having nothing in particular to mark it. All the Pipeworks tunnels branched off from the main tunnel to the south, towards the city.

Arlin leaned towards Doon and shouted into his ear. 'First we'll go to the beginning of the river,' she said. She led him up the main tunnel for a long way. They passed other people in yellow slickers, who greeted Arlin with a nod and glanced curiously at Doon. After fifteen minutes or so, they came to the east edge of the Pipeworks, where the river surged up from a deep chasm in the ground, churning so violently that its dark water turned white and filled the air with a spray that wet Doon's face.

In the wall to their right was a wide double door. 'See that door right there?' Arlin shouted, pointing.

'Yes,' Doon shouted back.

'That's the generator room.'

'Can we go in?'

'Of course not!' said Arlin. 'You have to have special permission.' She pointed back down the main tunnel. 'Now we'll go to the end of the river,' she said.

She led him back, past the stairway door, all the way to the west edge of the Pipeworks. There the river flowed into a huge opening in the wall and vanished into darkness.

'Where does it go?' Doon asked.

Arlin just shrugged. 'Back into the ground, I guess. Now let's find Tunnel ninety-seven and get to work.' She pulled a folded piece of paper from her pocket. 'This is the map,' she said. 'You have one in your pocket, too. You have to use the map to find your way around in here.' The map looked to Doon like an immense centipede – the river arched across the top of the page like the centipede's body, and the tunnels dangled down from it like hundreds of long, long legs all tangled up with each other.

To get to Tunnel 97, they followed a complicated route through passageways lined with crusty, rusted pipes that carried water to all the buildings of Ember. Puddles stood on the floor of the tunnel, and water dripped in brown rivulets down the walls. Just as in the main tunnel, there was a string of bulbs along the ceiling that provided dim light. Doon occupied his mind by calculating how far underground he was. From the river to the ceiling of the main tunnel must be thirty feet or so, he thought. Above that were the storerooms, which occupied a layer at least twenty feet high. So that meant he was fifty feet underground, with tons of earth and rock and buildings above him. The thought made him tense up his shoulders. He cast a quick glance upwards, as if all that weight might collapse onto his head.

'Here we are,' said Arlin. She was standing next to a leak that spurted a stream of water straight out from the wall. 'We have to turn the shut-off valve, take the pipe apart, put on a new connector and stick it back together again.'

With wrenches, hammers, washers and black goop, they did this, getting soaked in the process. It took them most of the morning and proved to Doon that the city was in even worse shape than he'd suspected. Not only were the lights about to fail and the supplies about to run out, but the water system was breaking down. The whole city was crumbling, and what was anyone doing about it?

When the lunch break came, Arlin took her lunch sack from a pocket in her tool belt and went off to meet some friends a few tunnels away. 'You stay right here and wait until I get back,' she said as she left. 'If you wander around, you'll get lost.'

But Doon set out as soon as she disappeared. Using his map, he found his way back to the main tunnel, then hurried to the east end. He wasn't going to wait for special permission to see the generator. He was pretty sure he could find a way to get in on his own, and he did. He simply stood by the door and waited for someone to come out. Quite soon, a stout woman carrying a lunch sack pushed open the door and walked away. She didn't notice him. Before the door could close again, Doon slipped inside.

Such a horrendous noise met him that he staggered backwards a few steps. It was an earsplitting, growling, grinding, screaming noise, shot through with a hoarse *rackety-rackety* sound and underscored with a deep *chugga-chugga-chugga*. Doon clapped his hands over his ears and stepped forward. In front of him was a gigantic black machine, two storeys high. It was vibrating so hard it looked as if it might explode any second. Several people wearing earmuffs were busy around it. None of them noticed him come in.

He tapped one of them on the shoulder, and the person jumped and whirled round. He was an old man, Doon saw, with a deeply lined brown face.

'I want to learn about the generator!' Doon screamed, but he might as well have saved his breath. No one could be heard in the uproar. The old man glared at him, made a shooing motion with his hand and turned back to work.

Doon stood and watched for a while. Beside the huge machine were ladders on wheels that the workers pushed back and forth and climbed up on to reach the high parts. All over the room, greasy-looking cans and tools littered the floor. Against the walls stood big bins holding every kind of bolt and screw and gear and lever and rod and tube, all of them black with age and jumbled together. The workers scurried between the bins and the generator or simply stood and watched the thing shake.

After a few minutes, Doon left. He was horrified. All his life he had studied how things worked – it was one of his favourite things to do. He could take apart an old watch and put it back together exactly as it had been. He understood how the taps in the sink worked. He'd fixed the toilet many times. He'd made a wheeled cart out of the parts of an old armchair. He even had a hazy idea of what was going on in the refrigerator. He was proud of his mechanical talent. There was only one thing he didn't understand at all, and that was electricity. What was the power that ran through the wires and into the light bulbs? Where did it come from? He had thought that if he could just get a look at the generator, he would have the clue he needed. From there, he could begin to work on a solution that would keep the lights of Ember burning.

But one glimpse of the generator showed him how foolish he was. He'd expected to see something whose workings he could understand – a wheel turning, a spark being struck, some wires that led from one point to another. But this monstrous roaring thing – he wondered if *anyone* understood how it worked. It looked as if all they were doing was trying to keep it from flying apart.

As it turned out, he was right. When the day was over and he was upstairs taking off his boots and slicker, he saw the old man from the generator room and went to talk to him. 'Can you explain to me about the generator?' he asked. 'Can you tell me how it works?'

The old man just sighed. 'All I know is, the river makes it go.'

'But how?'

The man shrugged. 'Who knows? Our job is just to keep it from breaking down. If a part breaks, we got to put on a new one. If a part freezes up, we got to oil it.' He wiped his hand wearily across his forehead, leaving a streak of black grease. 'I been working on the generator for twenty years. It's always managed to chug along, but this year . . . I don't know. The thing seems to break down every couple of minutes.' He cracked a wry smile. 'Of course, I hear we might run out of light bulbs before that, and then it won't matter if the generator works or not.'

Running out of light bulbs, running out of power, running out of time – disaster was right around the corner. That's what Doon was thinking about when he stopped outside the Gathering Hall on his way home and saw Lina on the roof. She looked so free and happy up there. He didn't know why she was on the roof, but he wasn't surprised. It was the kind of thing she did, turning up in unexpected places, and now that she was a messenger, she could go just about anywhere. But how could she be so lighthearted when everything was falling apart?

He headed for home. He lived with his father in a two-bedroom apartment over his father's shop in Greengate Square – the Small Items shop, which sold things like nails, pins, clips, springs, jar lids, doorknobs, bits of wire, shards of glass, chunks of wood and other small things that might be useful in some way. The Small Items shop had overflowed somewhat into their apartment above. In their front room, where other people might display a nice teapot on a tabletop or a few attractive squashes or tomatoes on a shelf, they had buckets and boxes and baskets full of spare items for the shop, things Doon's father had collected but not yet organized for selling. Often these items spilled over onto the floor. It was easy to trip over things in this apartment, and not a good idea to go barefoot.

Today Doon didn't stop in at the shop to see his father before going upstairs. He wasn't in the mood for conversation. He removed two buckets of stuff from the couch – it looked like mostly shoe heels – and flopped down on the cushions. He'd been stupid to think he could understand the generator just by looking at it, when other people had been working on it their entire lives. The thing was, he had to admit, he'd always thought he was smarter than other people. He'd been sure he could learn about electricity and help save the city. He wanted to be the one to do it. He had imagined many times a ceremony in

Harken Square, organized to thank him for saving Ember, with the entire population in attendance and his father beaming from the front row. All Doon's life, his father had been saying to him, 'You're a good boy and a smart boy. You'll do grand things some day, I know you will.' But Doon hadn't done much that was grand so far. He ached to do something truly important, like finding the secret of electricity and, as his father watched, be rewarded for his achievement. The size of the reward didn't matter. A small certificate would do, or maybe a badge to sew on his jacket.

Now he was stuck in the muck of the Pipeworks, patching up pipes that would leak and break again in a matter of days. It was even more useless and boring than being a messenger. The thought made him suddenly furious. He sat up, grabbed a shoe heel out of the bucket at this feet and hurled it with all his might. It arrived at the front door just as the door opened. Doon heard a hard *thwack* and a loud 'Ouch!' at the same moment. Then he saw the long, lean, tired-looking face of his father in the doorway.

Doon's anger drained away. 'Oh, I hit you, Father. I'm sorry.'

Doon's father rubbed the side of his head. He was a tall man, bald as a peeled potato, with a high forehead and a long chin. He had kind, slightly puzzled grey eyes.

'Got me in the ear,' he said. 'What *was* that?'

'I got angry for a second,' said Doon. 'I threw one of these old heels.'

'I see,' said his father. He brushed some bottle tops off a chair and sat down. 'Does it have to do with your first day at work, son?'

'Yes,' said Doon.

His father nodded. 'Why don't you tell me about it,' he said.

Doon told him. When he was finished, his father ran a hand across his bald head as if smoothing down the hair that wasn't there. He sighed. 'Well,' he said, 'it sounds unpleasant, I have to admit. About the generator, especially – that's bad news. But the Pipeworks is your assignment, no way around it. What you get is what you get. What you *do* with what you get, though . . . that's more the point, wouldn't you say?' He looked at Doon and smiled, a bit sadly.

'I guess so,' Doon said. 'But what can I do?'

'I don't know,' said his father. 'You'll think of something. You're a clever boy. The main thing is to pay attention. Pay close attention to everything, notice what no one else notices. Then you'll know what no one else knows, and that's always useful.' He took off his coat and hung it from a peg on the wall. 'How's the worm?' he asked.

'I haven't looked at it yet,' said Doon. He went into his room and came out with a small wooden box covered with an old scarf. He set the box on the table and took the scarf off, and he and his father both bent over to look inside.

A couple of limp cabbage leaves lay on the bottom of the box. On one of the leaves was a worm about an inch long. A few days before school ended, Doon had found the worm on the underside of a cabbage leaf he was slicing up for dinner. It was a pale soft green, velvety smooth all over, with tiny stubby legs.

Doon had always been fascinated by bugs. He wrote down his observations about them in a book he had titled *Crawling and Flying Things*. Each page of the book was divided lengthwise down the centre. On the left he drew his pictures, with a pencil sharpened to a needle-like point: moth wings with their branching patterns of veins; spider legs, which had minute hairs and tiny feet like claws; beetles, with their feelers and their glossy armour. On the right, he wrote what he observed about each creature. He noted what it ate, where it slept, where it laid its eggs and – if he knew – how long it lived.

This was difficult with fast-moving creatures like moths and spiders. To learn anything about them, he had to catch what glimpses he could as they lived their lives out in the open. If he put them in a box, they scrambled around for a few days and then died.

This worm, though, was different. It seemed perfectly happy to live in the box Doon had made for it.

So far, it did only three things: eat, sleep (it looked like sleeping, though Doon couldn't tell if the worm closed its eyes – or even if it had eyes) and expel tiny black poop balls. That was it.

'I've had it for five days now,' said Doon. 'It's twice as big as it was when I got it. It's eaten two square inches of cabbage leaf.'

'You're writing all this down?'

Doon nodded.

'Maybe,' said his father, 'you'll find some interesting new bugs in the Pipeworks.'

'Maybe,' said Doon. But to himself he said, No, that's not enough. I can't go plodding around the Pipeworks, stopping up leaks, looking for bugs and pretending there's no emergency. I have to find something important down there, something that's going to help. I have to. I just *have* to.

CHAPTER 4

Something Lost, Nothing Found

One day when Lina had been a messenger for several weeks, she came home to find that Granny had thrown all the cushions from the couch onto the floor, ripped up a corner of the couch's lining, and was pulling out wads of stuffing.

'What are you doing?' Lina cried.

Granny looked up. Wisps of sofa stuffing stuck to the front of her dress and clung to her hair. 'Something is lost,' she said. 'I think it might be in here.'

'What's lost, Granny?'

'I don't quite recall,' said the old woman. 'Something important.'

'But Granny, you're ruining the couch. What will we sit on?'

Granny tore a bit more of the covering off the couch and yanked out another puff of stuffing. 'It doesn't matter,' she said. 'I'll put it back together later.'

'Let's put it back now,' Lina said. 'I don't think what's lost is in there.'

'You don't know,' said Granny darkly. But she sat back on her heels, looking tired.

Lina began cleaning up the mess. 'Where's the baby?' she asked.

Granny gazed at Lina blankly. 'The baby?'

'You haven't forgotten the baby?'

'Oh, yes. She's . . . I think she's down in the shop.'

'By herself?' Lina stood up and ran down the stairs. She found Poppy sitting on the floor of the shop, enmeshed in a tangle of yellow yarn. As soon as she saw Lina, Poppy began to howl.

Lina picked her up and unwound the yarn, talking soothingly, though she was so upset that her fingers trembled. For Granny to forget the baby was dangerous. Poppy could fall downstairs and hurt herself. She could wander out into the street and get lost. Granny had been forgetful lately, but this was the first time she'd completely forgotten about Poppy.

When they got upstairs, Granny was kneeling on the floor gathering up the white tufts of stuffing and jamming them back into the hole she'd made in the couch. 'It wasn't in there,' she said sadly.

'*What* wasn't?'

'It was lost a long time ago,' said Granny. 'My father told me about it.'

Lina sighed impatiently. More and more, her

grandmother's mind seemed caught in the past. She could explain the rules of pebblejacks, which she'd last played when she was eight, or tell you what happened at the Singing when she was twelve, or who she'd danced with at the Cloving Square Dance when she was sixteen, but she would forget what had happened the day before yesterday.

'They heard him talking about it when he died,' she said to Lina.

'They heard who talking?'

'My grandfather. The seventh mayor.'

'And what did they hear him say?'

'Ah,' said her grandmother with a faraway look. 'That's the mystery. He said he couldn't get at it. "Now it is lost," he said.'

'But what *was* it?'

'He didn't say.'

Lina gave up. It didn't matter anyway. Probably the lost thing was the old man's left sock, or his hairbrush. But for some reason, the story had taken root in Granny's mind.

The next morning on her way to work, Lina stopped in at the house of their neighbour, Evaleen Murdo. Mrs Murdo was brisk in her manner, and in her person thin and straight as a nail, but she was kind in her unsmiling way. Until a few years ago, she'd run a shop that sold paper and pencils. But when paper and pencils became scarce, her shop closed.

Now she spent her days sitting by her upstairs window, watching people in the street with her sharp eyes. Lina told Mrs Murdo about her grandmother's forgetfulness. 'Will you look in on her sometimes and make sure things are all right?' she asked.

'I will, certainly,' said Mrs Murdo, nodding twice, firmly. Lina went away feeling better.

That day Lina was given a message by Arbin Swinn, who ran the Callay Street Vegetable Market, to be delivered to Lina's friend Clary, the greenhouse manager. Lina was glad to carry this message, though her gladness was mixed a little with sadness. Her father had worked in the greenhouses. It still felt strange not to see him there.

The five greenhouses produced all of Ember's fresh food. They were out past Greengate Square, at the farthest edge of the city. Nothing else was out there but the trash heaps, great mouldering, stinking hills that stood on rocky ground and were lit by a few floodlights high up on poles.

It used to be that no one went to the trash heaps but the trash collectors, who dumped the trash and left it. Now and then a couple of children might go there to play, scrambling up the side of the heaps and tumbling down. Lina and Lizzie used to go when they were younger. They'd pull out the occasional treasure – some empty cans, maybe an old hat or a cracked plate. But not any more. Now there were guards posted at the trash heaps to make sure no one poked around. Just recently, an official job called trash sifter had been created. Every day a team of people methodically sorted through the trash heaps in search of anything that might be at all useful. They'd come back with broken chair legs that could be used for repairing window frames, bent nails that could become hooks for clothes, even filthy rags, stiff with dirt, that could be washed out and used to patch holes in window blinds or mattress covers. Lina hadn't thought about it before, but now she wondered about the trash sifters. Were they there because Ember really was running out of everything?

Beyond the trash heaps there was nothing at all – that is, only the vast Unknown Regions, where the darkness was absolute.

From the end of Diggery Street, Lina could see the long, low greenhouses. They looked like big tin cans that had been cut in half and laid on their sides. Her breath came a little faster. The greenhouses were a home to her, in a way.

She knew that she was most likely to find Clary somewhere around Greenhouse 1, where the office was, so that was where she headed first. A small tool-shed stood beside the door to Greenhouse 1; Lina peeked into it but saw only rakes and shovels. So she opened the greenhouse door. Warm, furry-smelling air washed over her, and all her love for this place came rushing back. Out of habit, she gazed up towards the ceiling, as if she might see her father there on his ladder, tinkering with the sprinkler system, the temperature gauges and the lights.

The greenhouse light was whiter than the yellowish light of the Ember streetlamps. It came from long tubes that ran the length of the ceiling. In this light, the leaves of the plants shone so green they almost hurt Lina's eyes. On the days when she'd come here with her father, Lina had spent hours wandering along the gravel paths that ran between the vegetable beds, sniffing the leaves, poking her fingers into the dirt, and learning to tell the plants apart by their look and smell. There were the beans and peas with their curly tendrils, the dark green spinach, the ruffled lettuce, and the hard, pale green cabbages, some of them as big a newborn baby's head. What she loved best was to rub the leaves of the tomato plant between her fingers and breathe in their pungent, powdery smell.

A long, straight path led from one end of the building to the other. About halfway down the path, Clary was crouching by a bed of carrots. Lina ran towards her, and Clary smiled, brushed the dirt from her hands and stood up.

Clary was tall and solid, with big hands and knobby knuckles. She had a square jaw and square shoulders, and brown hair cut in a short, squarish way. You might have thought from looking at her that she was a gruff, unfriendly person – but her nature was just the opposite. She was more comfortable with plants than with people, Lina's father had always said. She was strong but shy, a person of much knowledge but few words. Lina had always liked her. Even when she was little, Clary did not treat her like a baby but gave her jobs to do – pulling up carrots, picking bugs off cabbages. Since her parents had died, Lina had come many times to talk to Clary, or just to work silently beside her. Clary was always kind to her, and working with the plants took Lina's mind off her grief.

'Well,' said Clary. She smiled at Lina, wiped her hands on her already grimy pants, and smiled some more. Finally she said, 'You're a messenger.'

'Yes,' said Lina, 'and I have a message for you. It's from Arbin Swinn. "Please add four extra crates to my order, two of potatoes and two of cabbages."'

Clary frowned. 'I can't do that,' she said. 'At least, I can send him the cabbages, but only one small crate of potatoes.'

'Why?' asked Lina.

'Well, we have a sort of problem with the potatoes.'

'What is it?' asked Lina. Clary had a habit of answering questions in the briefest possible way. You had to keep asking and asking before she would believe you really wanted to know and weren't just being polite. Then she would explain, and you could see how much she knew, and how much she loved her work.

'I'll show you,' she said. She led the way to a bed where the green leaves were spotted with black. 'A new disease. I haven't seen it before. When you dig up the potatoes, they're runny inside instead of hard, and they stink. I'm going to have to throw out all the ones in this bed. There are only a few beds left that aren't infected.'

Most people in Ember had potatoes at every meal – mashed, boiled, stewed, roasted. They'd had fried potatoes, too, in the days before the cooking oil ran out.

'I'd hate it if we couldn't have potatoes any more,' Lina said.

'I would, too,' said Clary.

They sat on the edge of the potato bed and talked for a while, about Lina's grandmother and the baby, about the trouble Clary was having with the beehives, and about the greenhouse sprinkler system. 'It hasn't worked right since . . .' Clary hesitated and glanced sideways at Lina. 'For a long time,' she said. She didn't want to say 'since your father died'. Lina understood that.

She stood up. 'I should go,' she said. 'I have to take Arbin Swinn the answer to his message.'

'I hope you'll come again,' said Clary. 'You can come whenever . . . you can come any time.' Lina said thank you and turned to go.

But just outside the greenhouse door, she heard running footsteps and a strange, high, sobbing sound. Or rather, she heard sobs and then a wail, sobs and then a shout, and then more sobs, getting louder. She looked back towards the rear of the greenhouses, towards the trash heaps. 'Clary,' she called. 'There's something . . .'

Clary came out and listened, too.

'Do you hear it?'

'Yes,' said Clary. She frowned. 'I'm afraid it's . . . it's someone who . . .' She peered towards the crying noise. 'Yes . . . here he comes.' Her strong hand gripped Lina's shoulder for a moment. 'You'd better go,' she said. 'I'll take care of this.'

'But what is it?'

'Never mind. Just go on.'

But Lina wanted to see. Once Clary had walked away, she ducked behind the toolshed. From there she watched.

The noise came closer. Out beyond the trash heaps, a figure appeared. It was a man, running and stumbling, his arms flopping. He looked as if he was about to fall over, as if he could hardly pick up his feet. In fact, as he came closer he *did* fall. He tripped over a hose and crumpled to the ground as if his bones had dissolved.

Clary stooped down and said something to him in a voice too low for Lina to hear.

The man was panting. When he turned over and sat up, Lina saw that his face was scratched and his eyes wide open in fright. His sobs had turned into hiccups. She recognized him. It was Sadge Merrall, one of the clerks in the Supply Depot. He was a quiet, long-faced man who always looked worried.

Clary helped him to his feet. The two of them came slowly towards the greenhouse, and as they got closer Lina could hear what the man was saying. He spoke very fast in a weak, trembly voice, hardly stopping for breath. '. . . was sure I could do it. I said to myself, Just one step after another, that's all, one step after another. I knew it would be dark. Who doesn't know that? But I thought, Well, dark can't hurt you. I'll just keep going, I thought . . .'

He stumbled and sagged against Clary. 'Careful,' Clary said. They reached the door of the greenhouse, and Clary struggled to open it. Without thinking, Lina darted out from behind the toolshed and opened it for her. Clary shot her a quick frown but said nothing.

Sadge didn't stop talking. '. . . But then the farther I went the darker it was, and you can't just keep walking into black dark, can you? It's like a wall in front of you. I kept turning round to look at the lights of the city, because that's all there was to see, and then I'd say to myself, Don't look back, keep moving. But I kept tripping and falling... The ground is rough out there, I scraped my hands.' He held up one hand and stared at the red scratches on it, which oozed drops of blood.

They got him into Clary's office and sat him down in her chair. He rambled on.

'Be brave, I said to myself. I kept going and going, but then all of a sudden I thought, Anything could be out here! There could be a pit a thousand feet deep right in front of me. There could be . . . something that bites. I've heard stories . . . rats as big as garbage bins . . . And I had to get out of there. So I turned round and I ran.'

'Never mind,' said Clary. 'You're all right now. Lina, get him some water.'

Lina found a cup and filled it from the sink in the corner. Sadge took it with a shaking hand and drank it down.

'What were you looking for?' Lina asked. She knew what *she* would have been looking for if she'd gone out there. She'd thought about it countless times.

Sadge stared at her. He seemed to have to puzzle over her question. Finally he said, 'I was looking for something that could help us.'

'What would it be?'

'I don't know. Like a stairway that leads somewhere, maybe. Or a building full of . . . I don't know,
useful things.'

'But you didn't find anything? Or see anything?'
Lina asked, disappointed.

'Nothing! Nothing! There is nothing out there!'
His voice became a shout and his eyes looked wild
again. 'Or if there is, we can never get to it. Never! Not
without a light.' He took a long, shaky breath. For a
while he stared at the floor. Then he stood up. 'I think
I'm all right now. I'll be going.'

With uncertain steps, he went down the path and
out the door.

'Well,' said Clary. 'I'm sorry that happened while
you were here. I was afraid you might be scared, that's
why I told you to go.'

But Lina was full of questions, not fear. She had
heard tales of people who tried to go out into the
Unknown Regions. She had thought about it herself –
in fact, she'd wondered the same things as Sadge. She
had imagined making her way out into the dark and
coming to a wall in which she would find the door to
a tunnel, and at the end of the tunnel would be the
other city, the city of light that she had dreamed
about. All it would take was the courage to walk away
from Ember and into the darkness, and then to keep
going.

It might have been possible if you could carry a

light to show the way. But in Ember, there was no such thing as a light you could carry with you. Outside lights were fixed to their poles, or to the roofs of houses; inside lights were set into the ceiling or had cords that had to be plugged in. Over the course of Ember's history, various clever people had tried to invent a moveable light, but all of them had failed. One man had managed to ignite the end of a stick of wood by holding it against the electric burner on his stove. He'd run across the city with the flaming stick, planning to use it to light his journey. But by the time he got to the trash heaps, his torch had gone out. Other people latched onto his idea – one woman who lived on Dedlock Street, very near the edge of the city, managed to get into the Unknown Regions with her flaming stick. But the stick burned quickly, and before she could go far, the flame singed her hands and she threw it down. Everyone who had tried to penetrate the Unknown Regions had come back within a few hours, their enterprise a failure.

Lina and Clary stood by the open door of the greenhouse and watched Sadge shuffle towards the city. As he neared the trash heaps, two guards who had been sitting on the ground got to their feet. They walked over to Sadge, and each of them took hold of one of his arms.

'Uh-oh,' said Clary. 'Those guards are always looking for trouble.'

'But Sadge hasn't broken any law,' said Lina.

'Doesn't matter. They need something to do. They'll get some fun out of scaring him.' One of the guards was shaking his finger at Sadge and saying something in a voice almost loud enough for Lina to hear. 'Poor man,' said Clary with a sigh. 'He's the fourth one this year.'

The guards were marching Sadge away now, one on either side of him. Sadge looked limp and small between them.

'What do you think is out in the Unknown Regions, Clary?'

Clary stared down at the ground, where the light from the greenhouse was casting long, thin shadows of them both. 'I don't know. Nothing, I guess.'

'And do you think Ember is the only light in the dark world?'

Clary sighed. 'I don't know,' she said. She gave Lina a long look. Her eyes, Lina thought, looked a little sad. They were a deep brown, almost the colour of the earth in the garden bed.

Clary put a hand in her pocket and drew something out. 'Look,' she said. In the palm of her hand was a white bean. 'Something in this seed knows how to make a bean plant. How does it know that?'

'I don't know,' said Lina, staring at the hard, flat bean.

'It knows because it has life in it,' said Clary. 'But

where does life come from? What *is* life?'

Lina could see that words were welling up in Clary now; her eyes were bright, her cheeks were rosy.

'Take a lamp, for instance. When you plug it in, it comes alive, in a way. It lights up. That's because it's connected to a wire that's connected to the generator, which is making electricity, though don't ask me how. But a bean seed isn't connected to anything. Neither are people. We don't have plugs and wires that connect us to generators. What makes living things go is *inside* them somehow.' Her dark eyebrows drew together over her eyes. 'What I mean is,' she said finally, 'something is going on that we don't understand. They say the Builders made the city. But who made the Builders? Who made *us*? I think the answer must be somewhere outside of Ember.'

'In the Unknown Regions?'

'Maybe. Maybe not. I don't know.' She brushed her hands together in a time-to-get-back-to-work way.

'Clary,' said Lina quickly, 'here's what I think.' Her heart sped up. She hadn't told this to anyone before. 'In my mind, I see another city.' Lina watched to see if Clary was going to laugh at her, or smile in that overly kind way. She didn't, so Lina went on. 'It isn't like Ember; it's white and gleaming. The buildings are tall and sort of sparkle. Everything is bright, not just inside the buildings but all around them, too, even up in the sky. I know it's just my imagination, but it feels real. I think it *is* real.'

Clary said, 'Hmmm,' and then she said, 'Where would such a city be?'

'That's what I don't know. Or how to get to it. I keep thinking there's a door somewhere, maybe out in the Unknown Regions — a door that leads out of Ember, and then behind the door a road.'

Clary just shrugged her shoulders. 'I don't know,' she said. 'I have to get back to work. But here — take this.' She handed Lina the bean seed, took a little pot from a shelf, scooped some dirt into it and handed the pot to Lina, too. 'Stick the bean in here and water it every day,' she said. 'It looks like nothing, like a little white stone, but inside it there's life. That must be a sort of clue, don't you think? If we could just figure it out.'

Lina took the seed and the pot. 'Thank you,' she said. She wanted to give Clary a hug but didn't, in case it would embarrass her. Instead, she just said goodbye and raced back towards the city.

CHAPTER 5

On Night Street

Granny's mind was getting more and more muddled. Lina would come home in the evenings and find her rifling through the kitchen cupboards, surrounded by cans and jars with their lids off, or tearing the covers off her bed and trying to lift up the mattress with her skinny arms. 'It was an important thing,' she would say, 'the thing that was lost.'

'But if you don't know what it was,' said Lina, 'how will you know when you've found it?'

Granny didn't try to answer this question. She just flapped her hands at Lina and said, 'Never mind, never mind, never mind,' and kept on searching.

These days, Mrs Murdo spent a great deal of time sitting by their window rather than her own. She would tell Granny she was just coming to keep her company. 'I don't want her to keep me company,' Granny complained to Lina, and Lina said, 'Maybe she's lonely, Granny. Let her come.'

Lina rather liked having Mrs Murdo around – it was a bit like having a mother there. She wasn't anything like Lina's own mother, who had been a dreamy, absent-minded sort of person. Mrs Murdo was mother-like in quite a different way. She made sure they all ate a good breakfast in the morning – usually potatoes with mushroom gravy and beet tea. She lined up the vitamin pills by each person's plate and made sure they were swallowed. When Mrs Murdo was there, shoes got picked up and put away, spills were wiped off the furniture, and Poppy always had on clean clothes. Lina could relax when Mrs Murdo was around. She knew things were taken care of.

Every week, Lina – like all workers between age twelve and age fifteen – had Thursday off. One Thursday, as she was standing in line at the Garn Square market, hoping to get a bag of turnips for stew that night, she overheard a startling conversation between two people standing behind her.

'What I wanted,' said one voice, 'was some paint for my front door. It hasn't been painted for years. It's grey and peeling, horrible. I heard a store over on Night Street had some. I was hoping for blue.'

'Blue would be nice,' said the other voice wistfully.

'But when I got there,' the first voice continued, 'the man said he had no paint, never had. Disagreeable man. All he had were a few coloured pencils.'

Coloured pencils! Lina had not seen coloured pencils in any store for ages. Once she'd had two red ones, a blue one and a brown one. She'd used these for her drawing until they were stubs too small to hold. Now she had only one plain pencil left, and it was rapidly growing shorter.

She longed to have coloured pencils for her pictures of the imaginary city. She had a feeling it was a colourful place, though she didn't know what its colours might be. There were other things, of course, on which her money would be better spent. Granny's only coat was full of holes and coming apart at the seams. But Granny rarely went out, Lina told herself. She was either at home or in her yarn shop. She didn't really need a new coat, did she? Besides, how much could a few pencils cost? She could probably get a coat for Granny *and* some pencils.

So that afternoon she set out for Night Street. She took Poppy with her. Poppy had learned how to ride piggyback – she wrapped her legs around Lina's waist and gripped Lina's throat with her small, strong fingers.

On Budloe Street, people were standing in long lines with their bundles of laundry at the washing stations. The washers stirred the clothes in the washing machines with long poles. In days past, the machines themselves had whirled the clothes around, but not one of them worked any more.

On Night Street

Lina turned up Hafter Street, where the four streetlamps were still out and a building crew was repairing a partly collapsed roof. Orly Gordon called out to her from high on a ladder, and Lina looked up and waved. Farther on, she passed a woman with bits of rope and string for sale and a man pulling a cart full of carrots and beets to the grocery stores. At the corner, a cluster of little children played catch with a rag ball. The streets were alive with people today. Moving fast, Lina threaded her way among them.

But as she went into Otterwill Street, she saw something that made her slow down. A man was standing on the steps of the Gathering Hall, shouting and howling, and a crowd of people had gathered around him. Lina went closer, and when she saw who it was, her insides gave a lurch. It was Sadge Merrall. His arms flailed wildly, and his eyes were stretched wide open. In a high, rapid voice, he wailed out a stream of words: 'I have been to the Unknown Regions!' he cried. 'There is nothing, nothing, nothing there! Did you think something out there might save us? Ha! There's only darkness and monsters, darkness and terrible deep holes, darkness for ever! The rats are the size of houses! The rocks are sharp as knives! The darkness sucks your breath out! No hope for us out there, oh no! No hope, no hope!' He went on like this for a few minutes and then crumpled to the ground. The people watching him looked at each other and shook their heads.

'Gone mad,' Lina heard someone say.

'Yes, completely,' said someone else.

Suddenly Sadge sprang up again and resumed his terrible shouting. The crowd stepped back. Some of them hurried away. A few of them approached Sadge, speaking in calming voices. They took him by the arms and led him, still shouting, down the steps.

'Who dat? Who dat?' said Poppy in her small, piercing voice.

Lina turned away from the miserable spectacle. 'Hush, Poppy,' she said. 'It's a poor, sad man. He doesn't feel good. We mustn't stare.'

She headed towards Night Street, which ran along Greengate Square. There a stringy-haired man sat cross-legged on the ground playing a flute made out of a drainpipe, and five or six Believers circled him, clapping and singing. 'Soon, soon, coming soon,' they sang. What's coming soon? Lina wondered, but she didn't stop to ask.

Two blocks beyond, she came to a store that had no sign in its window. This must be the one, she thought.

At first it looked closed. Its window was dark. But the door opened when she pushed on it, and a bell attached to its doorknob clanked. From the back room came a black-haired man with big teeth and a long neck. 'Yes?' he said.

Lina recognized him. He was the one who'd given her the message for the mayor on her very first day of work. His name was Hooper – no, Looper, that was it.

'Do you have pencils for sale?' she asked. It seemed doubtful. The shop's shelves were empty except for a few stacks of used paper.

Poppy squirmed on Lina's back and whimpered a little.

'Sometimes,' said Looper.

Poppy's whimper became a wail.

'All right, you can get down,' Lina said to her. She set her on the floor, where she tottered about unsteadily.

'What I'd like to see,' said Lina, 'are your coloured pencils. If you have any.'

'We have a few,' said Looper. 'They are somewhat expensive.' He smiled, showing his pushy teeth.

'Could I see them?' said Lina.

He went into the back room and returned a moment later, carrying a small box, which he set down on the counter. He took the lid off. Lina bent forward to look.

Inside the box were at least a dozen coloured pencils – red, green, blue, yellow, purple, orange. They had never even been sharpened; their ends were flat. They had erasers. Lina's heart gave a few fast beats.

'How much are they?' she said.

'Probably too much for you,' the man said.

'Probably *not*,' said Lina. 'I have a job.'

'Good, good,' the man said, smiling again. 'No need to take offence.' He picked up the yellow pencil and twirled it between his fingers. 'Each pencil,' he said, 'five dollars.'

Five dollars! For seven, you could buy a coat – it would be an old, patched coat, but still warm. 'That's too much,' Lina said.

He shrugged and began to put the lid back on the box.

'But maybe . . .' Lina's thoughts raced. 'Let me look at them again.'

Once more the man lifted the lid and Lina bent over the pencils. She picked one up. It was painted a deep clear blue, and on its flat top was the blue dot of the lead. The pink eraser was held on by a shiny metal collar. So beautiful! I could buy just one, Lina thought. Then I could save a little more and buy a coat for Granny *next* month.

'Make up your mind,' said the man. 'I have other customers who are interested, if you aren't.'

'All right. I'll take one. No, wait.' It was like hunger, what she felt. It was the same as when her hand sometimes seemed to reach out by itself to grab a piece of food. It was too strong to resist. 'I'll take two,' she said, and a faint, dazzly feeling came over her at the thought of what she was doing.

'Which two?' the man said.

There were more colours in that box of pencils than in all of Ember. Ember's colours were all so much the same – grey buildings, grey streets, black sky; even the colours of people's clothes were faded from long use into mud-green, and rust-red, and grey-blue. But these colours – they were as bright as the leaves and flowers in the greenhouse.

Lina's hand hovered over the pencils. 'The blue one,' she said. 'And . . . the yellow one – no, the . . . the . . .'

The man made an impatient noise in the back of his throat.

'The green one,' said Lina. 'I'll take the blue and the green.' She lifted them out of the box. She took the money from the pocket of her coat and handed it to the man, and she put the pencils in her pocket. They were hers now; she felt a fierce, defiant joy. She turned to go, and that was when she saw that the baby was no longer in the store.

'Poppy!' she cried. She whirled round. 'Did you see my little sister go out?' she asked the man. 'Did you see which way she went?'

He shrugged. 'Didn't notice,' he said.

Lina darted into the street and looked in both directions. She saw lots of people, some children, but no Poppy. She stopped an old woman. 'Have you seen a little girl, a baby, walking by herself? In a green jacket, with a hood?' The old woman just stared at her with dull eyes and shook her head.

'Poppy!' Lina called. 'Poppy!' Her voice rose to a shout. Such a little baby couldn't have gone far, she thought. Maybe down towards Greengate Square, where there were more people walking around. She began to run.

And then the lights flickered, and flickered again, and went out. Darkness slammed up in front of her like a wall. She stumbled, caught herself and stood still. She could see absolutely nothing.

Shouts of alarm came from up and down the street, and then silence. Lina stretched her arms out. Was she facing the street or a building? Terror swept through her. I must just stand still, she thought. The lights will come on again in a few seconds, they always do. But she thought of Poppy alone in the blackness, and her legs went weak. *I must find her.*

She took a step. When she didn't bump into any-thing, she took another step, and the fingers of her right hand crumpled against something hard. The wall of a building, she thought. Keeping her hand against it, she turned left a little and took another step forward. Then suddenly her hand touched empty air. This would be Dedlock Street. Or had she passed Dedlock Street already? She couldn't keep the picture of the streets clear in her mind. The darkness seemed to fill not just the city around her but the inside of her head as well.

Heart pounding, she waited. Come back, lights, she pleaded. Please come back. She wanted to call out to Poppy, to tell her to stand still, not to be afraid, she would come for her soon. But the darkness pressed against her and she couldn't summon her voice. She could hardly breathe. She wanted to claw the darkness away from her eyes, as if it were someone's hands.

Small sounds came from here and there around her – a whimpering, a shuffling. In the distance someone called out incoherently. How many minutes had gone by? The longest blackout ever had been three minutes and fourteen seconds. Surely this was longer.

She could have endured it if she'd been on her own. It was the thought of Poppy, lost, that she couldn't stand – and lost because she had been paying more attention to a box of pencils. Oh, she'd been selfish and greedy, and now she was so, so sorry! She made herself take another step forward. But then she thought, What if I'm going *away* from Poppy? She began to tremble, and she felt the sinking and dissolving inside her that meant she was going to cry. Her legs gave way like wet paper and she slid down until she was sitting on the street, with her head on her knees. Trembling, her mind a wordless whirl of dread, she waited.

An endless time went by. A moan came from somewhere to the left. A door slammed closed. Footsteps started, then stopped. Into Lina's mind floated the beginning of the worst question: What if the lights never . . . ? She squeezed her arms around her knees and made the question stop. Lights come back, she said to herself, Lights come back, come back.

And suddenly they did.

Lina sprang up. There was the street again, and people looking upwards with their mouths hanging open. All around, people started crying or wailing or grinning in relief. Then all at once everyone started to hurry, moving fast towards the safety of home in case it should happen again.

Lina ran towards Greengate Square, stopping everyone she passed. 'Did you see a little girl walking by herself just before the lights went out?' she asked. 'Green jacket with a hood?' But no one wanted to listen to her.

On the Bee Street side of the square stood a few people all talking at once and waving their arms. Lina ran up to them and asked her question.

They stopped talking and stared at her. 'How could we have seen anyone? The lights were out,' said Nammy Proggs, a tiny old woman whose back was so bent that she had to twist her head sideways to look up.

Lina said, 'No, she wandered away *before* the lights went out. She got away from me. She may have come this direction.'

'You have to keep your eye on a baby,' Nammy Proggs scolded.

'Babies need watching,' said one of the women who'd been singing with the Believers.

But someone else said, 'Oh, a toddler? Green jacket?' and he walked over to an open shop door and called, 'You have that baby in there?' and through the door came someone leading Poppy by the hand.

Lina dashed to her and lifted her up. Poppy broke into loud wails. 'You're all right now,' said Lina, holding her tightly. 'Don't worry, sweetie. You were just lost a moment, now you're all right. I've got you, don't worry.' When she looked up to thank the person who'd found her, she saw a face she recognized. It was Doon. He looked the same as when she'd last seen him, except that his hair was shaggier. He had on the same baggy brown jacket he always wore.

'She was marching up the street by herself,' he said. 'No one knew who she belonged to, so I took her into my father's shop.'

'She belongs to me,' Lina said. 'She's my sister. I was so afraid when she was lost. I thought she might fall and hurt herself, or be knocked over, or . . . Anyway, thank you *so much* for rescuing her.'

'Anyone would have,' said Doon. He frowned and looked down at the pavement.

Poppy had calmed down and was curled up against Lina's chest with her thumb in her mouth.

'And your job – how is it?' Lina asked. 'The Pipeworks?'

Doon shrugged his shoulders. 'All right,' he said. 'Interesting, anyway.'

She waited, but it seemed that was all he was going to say. 'Well, thank you again,' she said. She hoisted Poppy around to her back.

'Lucky for you Doon Harrow was around,' said Nammy Proggs, who'd been watching them with her sideways glare. 'He's a good-hearted boy. Anything breaks at my house, he fixes it.' She hobbled after Lina, shaking a finger at her. 'You'd better watch that baby more carefully,' she called.

'You shouldn't leave her alone,' the flute player added.

'I know,' said Lina. 'You're right.'

When she got home, she put the tired baby to bed in the bedroom they shared. Granny had been taking an afternoon nap in the front room and hadn't noticed the blackout at all. Lina told her that the lights had gone out for a few minutes, but she didn't mention anything about Poppy getting lost.

Later, in her bedroom, with Poppy asleep, she took the two coloured pencils from her pocket. They were not quite as beautiful as they had been. When she held them, she remembered the powerful wanting she had felt in that dusty store, and the feeling of it was mixed up with fear and shame and darkness.

CHAPTER 6

The Box in the Closet

It was strange how people didn't talk much about the blackout. Power failures usually aroused lively discussion, with clumps of people collecting on corners and saying to each other, 'Where were you when it happened?' and 'What's the matter with the electricians, we should kick them out and get new ones,' and that sort of thing. This time, it was just the opposite. When Lina went to work the next morning, the street was oddly silent. People walked quickly, their eyes on the ground. Those who did stop to talk spoke in low voices, then hurried on their way.

That day, Lina carried the same message twelve times. All the messengers were carrying it. It was simply this, being passed from one person to another: Seven minutes. The power failure had been more than twice as long as any other so far.

Fear had settled over the city. Lina felt it like a cold chill. She understood now that Doon had been speaking the truth on Assignment Day. Ember was in grave danger.

The next day a notice appeared on all the city's kiosks:

TOWN MEETING
ALL CITIZENS ARE REQUESTED TO ASSEMBLE
IN HARKEN SQUARE AT 6 P.M. TOMORROW
TO RECEIVE IMPORTANT INFORMATION.
MAYOR LEMANDER COLE

What kind of important information? Lina wondered. Good news or bad? She was impatient to hear it.

The next day, people streamed into Harken Square from all four directions, crowding together so close that each person hardly had room to move. Children sat on the shoulders of fathers. Short people tried to push towards the front. Lina spotted Lizzie and called a greeting to her. She saw Vindie Chance, too, who had brought her little brother. Lina had decided to leave Poppy at home with Granny. There was too much danger of losing her in a crowd like this.

The town clock began to strike. Six vibrating bongs rang out, and a murmur of anticipation swept through the crowd. People stood on tiptoe, craning to see. The door of the Gathering Hall opened, and the mayor came out, flanked by two guards. One of the guards handed the mayor a megaphone, and the mayor began to speak. His voice came through the megaphone both blurry and crackly.

'People of Ember,' he said. He waited. The crowd fell silent, straining to hear.

'People of Ember,' the mayor said again. He looked from side to side. The light glinted off his bald head. 'Our city has experienced some slight diff-cushlaylie. Times like this require gresh peshn frush all.'

'What did he say?' people whispered urgently. 'What did he say? I couldn't hear him.'

'Slight difficulties,' someone said. 'Requires great patience from us all.'

'But I stand here today,' the mayor went on, 'to reassure you. Difficult times will pass. We are mayg effn effuff.'

'What?' came the sharp whisper. 'What did he say?'

Those near the front passed word back. 'Making every effort,' they said. 'Every effort.'

'Louder!' someone shouted.

The mayor's voice blared through the megaphone louder but even less clear. 'Wursh poshuling!' he said. 'Pank. Mushen pank. No rrrshen pank.'

'We can't hear you!' someone else yelled. Lina felt a stirring around her, a muttering. Someone pushed against her back, forcing her forward.

'He said we mustn't panic,' someone said. 'He said panic is the worst possible thing. No reason to panic, he said.'

On the steps of the Gathering Hall, the two guards moved a little closer to the mayor. He raised the megaphone and spoke again.

'*Slooshns!*' he bellowed. '*Arbingfoun!*'

'Solutions,' the people in front called to the people in back. 'Solutions are being found, he said.'

'*What* solutions?' called a woman standing near Lina. People elsewhere in the crowd echoed what the woman had said. 'What solutions? What solutions?' Their cry became a chorus, louder and louder.

Again Lina felt the pressure from behind as people moved forward towards the Gathering Hall. Jostling arms poked her, bulky bodies bumped her and crushed her. Her heart began to pound. I have to get out of here! she thought.

She started ducking beneath arms and darting into whatever space she could find, making her way towards the rear of the crowd. Noise was rising everywhere. The mayor's voice kept coming in blasts of incomprehensible sound, and the people in the crowd were either shouting angrily or yelping in fear of being squashed. Someone stepped on Lina's foot, and her scarf was half yanked off. For a few seconds she was afraid she was going to be trampled. But at last she struggled free and ran up onto the steps of the school. From there she saw that the two guards were hustling the mayor back through the door of the Gathering Hall. The crowd roared, and a few people started hurling whatever they could find – pebbles, crumpled paper, even their own hats.

At the other side of the square, Doon and his father battled their way down Gilly Street. 'Move fast,' his father said. 'We don't want to be caught up in this crowd.' They crossed Broad Street and took the long way home, through the narrow lanes behind the school.

'Father,' said Doon as they hurried along, 'the mayor is a fool, don't you think?'

For a moment his father didn't answer. Then he said, 'He's in a tough spot, son. What would you have him do?'

'Not lie, at least,' Doon said. 'If he really has a solution, he should have told us. He shouldn't pretend he has solutions when he doesn't.'

Doon's father smiled. 'That would be a good start,' he agreed.

'It makes me so angry, the way he talks to us,' said Doon.

Doon's father put a hand on Doon's back and steered him towards the corner. 'A great many things make you angry lately,' he said.

'For good reason,' said Doon.

'Maybe. The trouble with anger is, it gets hold of you. And then you aren't the master of yourself any more. Anger is.'

Doon walked on silently. Inwardly, he groaned. He knew what his father was going to say, and he didn't feel like hearing it.

'And when anger is the boss, you get—'

'I know,' said Doon. 'Unintended consequences.'

'That's right. Like hitting your father in the ear with a shoe heel.'

'I didn't mean to.'

'That's exactly my point.'

They walked on down Pibb Street. Doon shoved his hands into the pockets of his jacket and scowled at the path. Father doesn't even *have* a temper, he thought. He's as mild as a glass of water. He can't possibly understand.

Lina was running. She'd already dismissed the mayor's speech from her mind. She sped by people on Otterwill Street going back to open their stores and overheard snatches of conversation as she passed. 'Expects us to believe . . .' said one voice. 'He's just trying to keep us quiet,' said another. '. . . Heading for disaster . . .' said a third. All the voices shook with anger and fear.

Lina didn't want to think about it. Her feet slapped the stones of the street, her hair flew out behind her. She would go home, she would make hot potato soup for the three of them, and then she would take out her new pencils and draw.

She climbed the stairs next to the yarn shop two at a time and burst through the door of the apartment. Something was on the floor just in front of her feet, and she tripped and fell down hard on her hands and knees. She stared. By the open closet door was a great pile of coats and boots and bags and boxes, their contents all spilled out and tangled up. A thumping and rattling came from inside the closet.

'Granny?'

More thumps. Granny's head poked round the edge of the closet door. 'I should have looked in here a long time ago,' she said. 'This is where it would be, of course. You should *see* what's in here!'

Lina gazed around at the incredible mess. Into this closet had been packed the junk of decades, jammed into cardboard boxes, stuffed into old pillowcases and laundry bags, and heaped up in a pile so dense that you couldn't pull one thing out without pulling all the rest with it. The shelf above the coatrack was just as crammed as the space below, mostly with old clothes that were full of moth holes and eaten away by mildew. When she was younger, Lina had tried exploring in this closet, but she never got far. She'd pull out an old scarf that would fall to pieces in her hands, or open a box that proved to be full of bent carpet tacks. Soon she would shove everything back in and give up.

But Granny was really doing the job right. She grunted and panted as she wrenched free the closet's packed-in stuff and tossed it behind her. It was clear that she was having fun. As Lina watched, a bag of rags came tumbling out the door, and then an old brown shoe with no laces.

'Granny,' said Lina, suddenly uneasy. 'Where's the baby?'

'Oh, she's here!' came Granny's voice from the depths of the closet. 'She's been helping me.'

Lina got up from the floor and looked around. She soon spotted Poppy. She was sitting behind the couch, in the midst of the clutter. In front of her was a small box made of something dark and shiny. It had a hinged lid, and the lid was open, hanging backwards.

'Poppy,' said Lina, 'let me see that.' She stooped down. There was some sort of mechanism on the edge of the lid – a kind of lock, Lina thought. The box was beautifully made, but it had been damaged. There were dents and scratches in its hard, smooth surface. It looked as if it had been a container for something valuable. But the box was empty now. Lina picked it up and felt around in it to be sure. There was nothing inside at all.

'Was there something in this box, Poppy? Did you

find something in here?' But Poppy only chortled happily. She was chewing on some crumpled paper. She had paper in her hands, too, and was tearing it. Shreds of paper were strewn around her. Lina picked one up. It was covered with small, perfect printing.

CHAPTER 7

A Message Full of Holes

It was the printing that sparked Lina's curiosity. It was not handwriting, or if it was, it was the neatest, most regular handwriting she had ever seen. It was more like the letters printed on cans of food or along the sides of pencils. Something other than a hand had written those words. A machine of some kind. This was the writing of the Builders. And so this piece of paper must have come from the Builders, too.

Lina gathered up the scraps of paper from the floor and gently pried open Poppy's fists and mouth to extract the crumpled wads. She put all this into the dented box and carried it to her room.

That evening, Granny and the baby were both asleep by a little after eight. Lina had nearly an hour to examine her discovery. She took the scraps from the box and spread them out on the table in her bedroom. The paper was thick; at each torn edge was a fringe of tangled fibres. There were many little pieces and one big piece with so many holes that it was like lace. The chewed bits were beyond saving – they were almost a paste. But Lina spread out the big lacy piece and saw that on one edge of it, which was still intact, was a column of numbers. She collected all the dry scraps and puzzled over them for a long time, trying to figure out where they fit into the larger piece. When she had arranged them as well as she could, this was what she had:

Instru   r Egres

This offic   doc   in
stric   secur   period of
  ears.

        prepara   made for
inha   city.
    as foll

1. Exp
   riv   ip   ork .
2.   ston   marked with E by r
   dge
3.   adde down   iverb nk
      to edge appr   eight
   low.
4.   acks to the
   wat r,   find door of bo

ker. Ke   hind small steel
pan   the right   . Rem
ey, open do .

5.   oat,   stocked with
nec   uip ent. Bac
ont   s   eet.

6. Usi   opes, lowe
ter. Head dow st   . Us pa
av   cks and assist over rap   .

7.   approx. 3 hours.
Disem
              . Follow   pat .

Lina could make sense of only a few words here
and there. Even so, something about this tattered document was exciting. It was not like anything Lina had
ever seen. She stared at the very first word at the top
of the page, 'Instru', and she suddenly knew what it
must be. She'd seen it often enough at school. It had
to be the beginning of 'Instructions'.

Her heart began knocking at her chest like a fist
at a door. She had found something. She had found
something strange and important: instructions for
something. But for what? And how terrible that
Poppy had found it first and ruined it!

It occurred to Lina that this might be what her
grandmother had been talking about for so long.

Perhaps *this* was the thing that was lost. But of course not knowing what had been lost, Granny wouldn't have recognized the box when she saw it. She would have tossed it out of the closet just as carelessly as she tossed everything else. Anyhow, it didn't matter whether this was the thing or not the thing. It was a mystery in itself, whatever it was, and Lina was determined to solve it.

The first step was to stick the scraps of paper down. They were so light that a breath could scatter them. She had a little bit of glue left in an old bottle. Painstakingly, she put a dot of glue on each of the scraps and pressed each one into its place on one of her precious few remaining whole sheets of paper. She put another piece of paper on top of this and set the box on top to flatten everything down. Just as she finished, the lights went out – she'd forgotten to keep an eye on the clock on her windowsill. She had to undress and get in bed in the dark.

She was too excited to sleep much that night. Her mind whirled around, trying to think what the message she'd found might be. She felt sure it had something to do with saving the city. What if these instructions were for fixing the electricity? Or for making a moveable light? That would change everything.

When the lights went on in the morning, she had a few minutes before Poppy wakened to work at the puzzle. But there were so many words missing! How could she ever make sense of such a jumble? As she pulled on her red jacket and tied the frayed and knotted laces of her shoes, she thought about it. If the paper was important, she shouldn't keep it to herself. But who could she tell? Maybe the messenger captain. She would know about things like official documents.

'Captain Fleery,' Lina said when she got to work, 'would you have time to come home with me later on today? Just for a minute? I found something I'd like to show you.'

'Found what?' asked Captain Fleery.

'Some paper with writing on it. I think it might be important.'

Captain Fleery raised her skinny eyebrows. 'What do you mean, important?'

'Well, I'm not sure. Maybe it isn't. But would you look at it anyway?'

So that evening Captain Fleery came home with Lina and peered at the bits of paper. She bent down and inspected the writing. 'Foll?' she said. 'Acks? Rem? Ont? What kind of words are those?'

'I don't know,' said Lina. 'The words are all broken up because Poppy chewed on them.'

'I see,' said Captain Fleery. She poked at the paper. 'This looks like instructions for something,' she said. 'A recipe, I suppose. "Small steel pan" – that would be what you use to cook it with.'

'But who would have such small, perfect writing?'

'That's the way they wrote in the old days,' said Captain Fleery. 'It could be a very *old* recipe.'

'But then why would it have been kept in this beautiful box?' She showed the box to Captain Fleery. 'I think it was locked up in here for some reason, and you wouldn't lock up something unless it was important . . . '

But Captain Fleery didn't seem to have heard her. 'Or,' she said, 'it could be a school exercise. Someone's homework that never got turned in.'

'But have you ever seen paper like this? Doesn't it look as if it came from someplace else – not here?'

Captain Fleery straightened up. A look of puzzlement came over her face. 'There *is* nowhere but here,' she said. She put both her hands on Lina's shoulders. 'You, my dear, are letting your imagination run away with you. Are you overtired, Lina? Are you anxious? I could put you on short days for a while.'

'No,' said Lina, 'I'm fine. I am. But I don't know what to do about . . . ' She gestured towards the paper.

'Never mind,' said Captain Fleery. 'Don't think about it. Throw it away. You're worrying too much – I know, I know, we all are, there's so much to worry about, but we mustn't let it unsettle us.' She gave Lina a long look. Her eyes were the colour of dishwater. 'Help is coming,' she said.

'Help?'

'Yes. Coming to save us.'

'Who is?'

Captain Fleery bent down and lowered her voice, as if telling a secret. 'Who built our city, dear?'

'The Builders,' said Lina.

'That's right. And the Builders will come again and show us the way.'

'They will?'

'Very soon,' said Captain Fleery.

'How do you know?'

Captain Fleery straightened up again and clapped a hand over her heart. 'I know it here,' she said. 'And I have seen it in a dream. So have all of us, all the Believers.'

So that's what they believe, Lina thought – and Captain Fleery is one of them. She wondered how the captain could feel so sure about it, just because she'd seen it in a dream. Maybe it was the same for her as the sparkling city was for Lina – she *wanted* it to be true.

The captain's face lit up. 'I know what you must do, dear – come to one of our meetings. It would lift your heart. We sing.'

'Oh,' said Lina, 'thank you, but I'm not sure I . . . maybe sometime . . .' She tried to be polite, but she knew she wouldn't go. She didn't want to stand around waiting for the Builders. She had other things to do.

Captain Fleery patted her arm. 'No pressure, dear,' she said. 'If you change your mind, let me know. But take my advice: forget about your little puzzle project. Lie down and take a nap. Clears the mind.' Her narrow face beamed kindness down at Lina. 'You take tomorrow off,' she said. She raised a hand good-bye and went down the stairs.

Lina took advantage of her day off to go to the Supply Depot to see Lizzie Bisco. Lizzie was quick and smart. She might have some good ideas.

At the Supply Depot, crowds of shopkeepers stood in long disorderly lines that stretched out the door. They pushed and jostled and snapped impatiently at each other. Lina joined them, but they seemed so frantic that they frightened her a little. They must be very sure now that the supplies are running out, she thought, and they're determined to get what they can before it's too late.

When she got close to the head of the line, she heard the same conversation several times. 'Sorry,' the clerk would say when a shopkeeper asked for ten packets of sewing needles, or a dozen drinking glasses, or twenty packages of light bulbs. 'There's a severe shortage of that item. You can have only one.' Or else the clerk would say, 'Sorry. We're out of that entirely.' 'For ever?' 'For ever.'

Lina knew that it hadn't always been this way. When Ember was a young city, the storerooms were full. They held everything the citizens could want – so much it seemed the supplies would never run out. Lina's grandmother had told her that schoolchildren were given a tour of the storerooms as part of their education. They took an elevator from the street level to a long, curving tunnel with doors on both sides and other tunnels branching off it. The guide led the tour down the long passages, opening one door after another. 'This area,' he would say, 'is Canned Goods. Next we come to School Supplies. And around this bend we have Kitchenware. Next come Carpentry Tools.' At each door, the children crowded against each other to see.

'Every room had something different,' Granny told Lina. 'Boxes of toothpaste in one room. Bottles of cooking oil. Bars of soap. Boxes of pills – there were twenty rooms just for vitamin pills. One room was stacked with hundreds of cans of fruit. There was something called pineapple, I remember that one especially.'

'What was pineapple?' asked Lina.

'It was yellow and sweet,' said Granny with a dreamy look in her eyes. 'I had it four times before we ran out of it.'

But these tours had been discontinued long before Lina was born. The storerooms, people said, were no longer a pleasure to look at. Their dusty shelves stood mostly empty now. It was rumoured

that in some rooms nothing was left at all. A child seeing the rooms where powdered milk had been stored,
or the rooms that stored bandages or socks or pins or
notebooks, or – most of all – the dozens of rooms that
had once held thousands of light bulbs – would not
feel, as earlier generations of children had, that Ember
was endlessly rich. Today's children, if they were to
tour the storerooms, would feel afraid.

Thinking about all this, Lina waited in the line of
people at Lizzie's station. When she got to the front,
she leaned forward with her elbows on the counter
and whispered, 'Lizzie, can you meet me after you're
through with work? I'll wait for you right outside the
door.' Lizzie nodded eagerly.

At four o'clock, Lizzie came trotting out the office
door. Lina said to her, 'Will you come home with me
for a minute? I want to show you something.'

'Sure,' said Lizzie, and as they walked, Lizzie
talked. 'My wrist is killing me from writing all day,'
she said. 'You have to write in the tiniest letters to save
paper, so I get a terrible *cramp* in my wrist and my
fingers. And people are so *rude*. Today they were
worse than ever. I said to some guy, "You can't have
fifteen cans of corn, you can only have three," and he
said, "Look, don't tell me that, I saw plenty of cans in
the Pott Street market just yesterday," and I said,
"Well, that's why there aren't so many left today," and
he said, "Don't be smart with me, carrot-head." But

what am I supposed to do? I can't *make* cans of corn out of thin air.'

They passed through Harken Square, around the Gathering Hall, and down Roving Street, where three of the floodlights were out, making a cave of shadow.

'Lizzie,' said Lina, interrupting the flow of talk. 'Is it true about light bulbs?'

'Is what true?'

'That there aren't very many left?'

Lizzie shrugged. 'I don't know. They hardly ever let us go downstairs into the storerooms. All we see are the reports the carriers turn in – how many forks in Room 1146, how many doorknobs in 3291, how many children's shoes in 2249 . . .'

'But when you see the report for the light bulb rooms, what does it say?'

'I never get to see that one,' said Lizzie. 'That one, and a few other ones like the vitamin report, only a few people can see.'

'Who?'

'Oh, the mayor, and of course old Flab Face.' Lina looked at her questioningly. 'You know, Farlo Batten, the head of the storerooms. He is so *mean*, Lina, you would just hate him. He counts us late if we come in even two minutes after eight, and he looks over our shoulders as we're writing, which is awful because he has bad breath, and he runs his finger over what we've written and says, "This word is illegible, that word is illegible, these numbers are illegible." It's his favourite word, illegible.'

When they came to Lina's street, Lina ducked her head in the door of the yarn shop and said hello to Granny, and then they climbed the stairs to the apartment. Lizzie was talking about how hard it was to stand up all day, how it made her knees ache, how her shoes pinched her feet. She stopped talking long enough to say hello to Evaleen Murdo, who was sitting by the window with Poppy on her lap, and then she began again as Lina led her into her bedroom.

'Lina, where were you when the big blackout came?' she asked, but she went right on without waiting for an answer. 'I was at home, *luckily*. But it was scary, wasn't it?'

Lina nodded. She didn't want to talk about what had happened that day.

'I hate those blackouts,' Lizzie went on. 'People say there's going to be more and more of them, and that some day—' She stopped, frowned and started again. 'Anyway, nothing bad happened to me. After that, I got up and figured out a whole new way to do my hair.'

It seemed to Lina that Lizzie was like a clock wound too tightly and running too fast. She'd always been a little this way, but today she was more so than ever. Her gaze skipped from one spot to another, her fingers twiddled with the edge of her shirt. She looked paler than usual, too. Her freckles stood out like little smudges of dirt on her nose.

'Lizzie,' said Lina, beckoning towards the table in the corner of her room. 'I want to show you—'

But Lizzie wasn't listening. 'You're so lucky to be a messenger, Lina,' she said. 'Is it fun? I wish I could have been one. I would have been so good at it. My job is so boring.'

Lina turned and looked at her. 'Isn't there *anything* you like about it?'

Lizzie pursed her lips in a tiny smile and looked sideways at Lina. 'There's one thing,' she said.

'What?'

'I can't tell you. It's a secret.'

'Oh,' said Lina. Then you shouldn't have mentioned it at all, she thought.

'Maybe I'll tell you someday,' said Lizzie. 'I don't know.'

'Well, I like *my* job,' Lina said. 'But what I wanted to talk to you about was what I found yesterday. It's this.'

She lifted the box away and took up the piece of paper covering the patched-together document. Lizzie gave it a quick look. 'Is it a message someone gave you? That got torn up?'

'No, it was in our closet. Poppy was chewing on it, that's why it's torn up. But look at the writing on it. Isn't it strange?'

'Uh-huh,' said Lizzie. 'You know who has beautiful handwriting? Myla Bone, who works with me. You should see it, it's got curly tails on the "y"s and the "g"s, and fancy loops on the capital letters. Of course Flab Face hates it, he says it's illegible . . .'

Lina slid the piece of paper back over the pasted-down scraps. She wondered why she had thought Lizzie would be interested in what she'd found. She'd always had fun with Lizzie. But their fun was usually with games – hide-and-seek, tag, the kinds of games where you run and climb. Lizzie never had been much interested in anything that was written on paper.

So Lina quietly put the document back in its place, and she sat down with Lizzie on the floor. She listened and listened until Lizzie's chatter ran down. 'I'd better go,' Lizzie said. 'It was fun to see you, Lina. I miss you.' She stood up. She fluffed her hair. 'What was it you wanted to show me? Oh, yes – the fancy writing. Really nice. Lucky you to find it. Come and see me again soon, all right? I get so bored in that office.'

Lina made beet soup for dinner that night, and Poppy spilled hers and made a red lake on the table. Granny stared into her bowl, stirring and stirring the soup with her spoon, but she didn't eat. She didn't feel quite right, she told Lina; after a while she wandered off to bed. Lina cleaned up the kitchen quickly. As soon as her chores were out of the way, she could get back to studying her document. She washed Poppy's clothes. She sewed on the buttons that had come off her messenger jacket. She picked up the rags and sacks and boxes and bags that Granny had tossed out of the closet. And by the time she had done all this and put Poppy to bed, she still had almost half an hour to study the fragments of paper.

She sat down at her desk and uncovered the document. With her elbows on either side of it and her chin resting in her hands, she pored over it. Though Lizzie and Captain Fleery had paid it no attention, Lina still thought this torn-up page must be important. Why else would it have been in such a cleverly fastened box? Maybe she should show it to the mayor, she thought reluctantly. She didn't like the mayor. She didn't trust him, either. But if this document was important to the future of the city, he was the one who should know about it. Of course, she couldn't ask the mayor to come to her house. She pictured him puffing up the stairs, squeezing through the door, looking disapprovingly at the clutter in their house, recoiling from Poppy's sticky hands – no, it wouldn't do.

But she didn't want to take her carefully patched-together document to the Gathering Hall, either. It was just too fragile. The best thing to do, she decided, was to write the mayor a note. She settled down to do this.

A Message Full of Holes

She found a fairly unspoiled half-piece of paper, and, using a plain pencil (she wasn't going to waste her coloured ones on the mayor), she wrote:

> Dear Mayor Cole,
>   I have discovered a document that was in the closet. It is instructions for something. I believe it is important because it is written in very old printing. Unfortunately it got chewed up by my sister, so it is not all there. But you can still read some bits of it, such as:
>
>   marked with E
>   find door of bo
>   small steel pan
>
>   I will show you this document if you want to see it.
>
>   Sincerely yours,
>   Lina Mayfleet, Messenger
>   34 Quillium Square

She folded the note in half and wrote 'Mayor Cole' on the front. On her way to work the next morning, she took it to the Gathering Hall. No one was sitting at the guard's desk, so Lina left the note there, placed so that the guard would see it when he arrived. Then, feeling that she had done her duty, she went off to her station.

* * *

Several days went by. The messages Lina carried were full of worry and fear. 'Do you have any extra Baby Drink? I can't find it at the store.' 'Have you heard what they're saying about the generator?' 'We can't come tonight – Grandpa B. won't get out of bed.'

Every day when she got home from work, Lina asked Granny, 'Did a message come for me?' But there was nothing. Maybe the mayor hadn't got her note. Maybe he'd got it and paid no attention. After a week, Lina decided she was tired of waiting. If the mayor wasn't interested in what she'd found, too bad for him. *She* was interested. She would figure it out herself.

Twice during the week, when Poppy and Granny were both asleep, she'd had a little free time. She'd spent this time making a copy of the document, in case anything happened to the fragile original. It had taken her a long time. She used one of her few remaining pieces of paper – an old label, slightly torn, from a can of peas. The copy was as accurate as she could make it, with the missing bits between the letters carefully indicated as dashes. She had tucked it under the mattress of her bed for safekeeping.

Now she finally had a whole free evening. Poppy and Granny were both asleep, and the apartment was tidy. Lina sat down at her table and uncovered the patched-together document. She tied back her hair so it wouldn't keep falling in her face, and she put a piece of paper next to her – blank except for a little bit of Poppy's scribbling – to write down what she decoded.

She started with the title. The first word she'd already figured out. It had to be *Instructions*. The next word could be *for*. Then came *Egres* – she wasn't sure about that. Maybe it was someone's name. Egresman. Egreston. Instructions for Egreston. She decided to call it *The Instructions* for short.

She went on to the first line. *This offic doc* probably meant *This official document*. Maybe *secur* meant *secure*. Or *security*. Then there were the words *period* and *ears* and *city*. But after that, so much was missing.

She studied the line next to the number 1. *Exp.* That could be *Expect* or *Expert* or so many things. She moved on to *riv*. That might be part of a word like *drive* or *strive*. What could *ip* and *ork* possibly be? They were so close together, maybe they were part of one word. What ended with *-ip*? *Whip*, Lina thought. *Trip. Slip.* What ended with *-ork*? *Fork* came to mind immediately. *Tripfork. Slipfork.* Nothing she could think of made sense.

Maybe it wasn't *fork*. What else ended in *-ork*? Starting at the beginning of the alphabet, Lina went through all the words that rhymed with *fork*. Most of them were nonsense: *bork, dork, gork, hork, jork* . . . This isn't going to work, she thought miserably. Oh . . . *work*! The word could be *work*.

Then what would the first part be? *Tripwork?* *Flipwork?* But maybe there was a letter between the p and the w. *Dipswork? Pipswork?*

Suddenly it came to her. Pipeworks. Pipeworks! That had to be it. Something in this message was about the Pipeworks!

Lina looked back at *Exp* and *riv. Riv!* That could be *river!* Rapidly she ran her eyes down the page. In line 3, she saw *iverb nk* – that looked like *riverbank.* The word *door* jumped out at her from line 4, whole on its scrap of paper. Lina took a quick breath. A door! What if it was the one she'd wished for, the one that led to the other city? Maybe her city was real after all, and these were instructions for finding it!

She wanted to leap from her chair and shout. The message had something to do with the river, a door and the Pipeworks. And who did she know who knew about the Pipeworks? Doon, of course.

She pictured his thin, serious face, and his eyes looking out searchingly from beneath his dark eyebrows. She pictured how he used to bend over his work at school, holding his pencil in a hard grip, and how, during free time, he was usually off by himself in a corner studying a moth or a worm or a taken-apart clock. That was one thing, at least, that she liked about Doon: he was curious. He paid attention to things.

And he cared about things, too. She remembered

how he'd been on Assignment Day, so furious at the mayor, so eager to trade his good job for her bad one so he could help save the city. And he'd taken Poppy inside his father's shop on the day of the blackout, so she wouldn't be afraid.

Why had she stopped being friends with Doon? She vaguely recalled the incident of the light pole. It seemed silly now, and long ago. The more she thought about Doon, the more it seemed he was the very person – the *only* person – who might be interested in what she had found.

She placed the plain sheet of paper over the Instructions and put the box on top. I'll go and find Doon, she thought. Tomorrow was Thursday – their day off. She would find him tomorrow and ask for his help.

CHAPTER 8

Explorations

Doon had taken to wandering the Pipeworks alone. He would go to his assigned tunnel and do his job quickly – once you got good at using your wrenches and brushes and tubes of glue, it wasn't hard. Most of the workers did their jobs quickly and then gathered in little groups to play cards or have salamander races or just talk and sleep.

But Doon didn't care about any of that. If he was going to be stuck in the Pipeworks, he would at least not waste the time he had. Since the long blackout, everything seemed more urgent than ever. Whenever the lights flickered, he was afraid the ancient generator might be shuddering to a permanent halt.

So while the others lounged around, he headed out towards the edges of the Pipeworks to see what he could see. 'Pay attention,' his father had said, and that's what he did. He followed his map when he could, but in some places the map was unclear. There were even tunnels that didn't show up on the map at all. To keep from getting lost, he dropped a trail of things as he walked – washers, bolts, pieces of wire, whatever he had in his tool belt – and then he picked them up on his way back.

His father had been at least a little bit right: there were interesting things in the Pipeworks if you paid attention. Already he had found three new crawling creatures: a black beetle the size of a pinhead, a moth with furry wings, and the best of all, a creature with a soft, shiny body and a small, spiral-patterned shell on its back. Just after he found this one, while he was sitting on the floor watching in fascination as the creature crept up his arm, a couple of workers came by and saw him. They burst into laughter. 'It's bug-boy!' one of them said. 'He's collecting bugs for his lunch!'

Enraged, Doon jumped up and shouted at them. His sudden motion made the creature fall off his arm to the ground, and Doon felt a crunch beneath his foot. The laughing workers didn't notice – they tossed a few more taunts at him and walked on – but Doon knew instantly what he'd done. He lifted his foot and looked at the squashed mess underneath.

Unintended consequences, he thought miserably. He was angry at his anger, the way it surged up and took over. He picked the bits of shell and goo off the sole of his boot and thought, I'm sorry. I didn't mean to hurt you.

In the days that followed, Doon went farther and farther into the Pipeworks, holding onto the hope that he might find something not only interesting but important. But what he found didn't seem important at all. Once he came upon an old pair of pliers that someone had dropped and left behind. Twice he found a coin. He discovered a supply closet that appeared to have been completely forgotten, but all it held were some boxes of plugs and washers and a rusty box containing shrivelled bits of what must once have been someone's lunch.

He found another supply closet at the far south end of the Pipeworks – at least, he assumed that's what it was. It was at the end of a tunnel with a rope strung across it; a sign hanging from the rope said, 'Caved In. No Entry'. Doon entered anyway, ducking under the rope. He found no sign of a cave-in, but there were no lights. He groped his way forward for twenty steps or so, and there the tunnel ended in a securely locked door – he couldn't see it, but he felt it. He retraced his steps, ducked back under the rope again, and walked on. A short distance away, he found a hatch in the ceiling of the tunnel – a square wooden panel that must lead, he thought, up into the storerooms. If he'd had something to stand on, he could have reached it and tried to open it, but it was about a foot above his upstretched hand. Probably it was locked anyhow. He wondered if the Builders had used openings like this one during the construction of the city to get more easily from one place to another.

On days when his job was near the main tunnel, he sometimes walked along the river after he'd finished working. He stayed away from the east end, where the generator was; he didn't want to think about the generator. Instead, he went the other way, towards the place where the river rushed out of the Pipeworks. The path grew less level at this end, and less smooth. The river here was bordered with clumps of wrinkled rock that seemed to grow out of the ground like fungus. Doon liked to sit on these clumps, running his fingers along the strange creases and crevices that must have been carved somehow by running or dripping water. In some places there were grooves that looked almost like writing.

But as for things of importance, Doon found none. It seemed that the Pipeworks was no use after all to a person who wanted to save the city. The generator was hopeless. He would never understand electricity. He used to think he could use electricity to invent a moveable light, if he studied hard enough. He took apart light bulbs; he took apart the electric outlets on the wall to see how the wires inside wound together and in the process got a painful, vibrating jolt all through his body. But when he tried to wind wires of his own together in exactly the same way, nothing happened. It was what came *through* the wires that made the light, he finally understood, and he had no idea what that was.

Now he could see only two courses of action: he could give up and do nothing, or he could start to work on a different kind of moveable light.

Doon didn't want to give up. So on his day off one Thursday, he went to the Ember Library to look up fire.

The library occupied an entire building on one side of Bilbollio Square. Its door was at the end of a short passage in the middle of the building. Doon went down the passage, pushed open the door and walked in. No one was there except for the librarian, ancient Edward Pocket, who sat behind his desk writing something with a tiny pencil clutched in his gnarled hand. The library had two big rooms, one for fiction, which was stories people made up out of their imaginations, and the other for fact, which was information about the real world. The walls of both rooms were lined with shelves, and on most of the shelves were hundreds of packets of pages. Each packet was held together with stout loops of string. The packets leaned against each other at angles and lay in untidy stacks. Some were thick, and some were so slim that only a clip was needed to hold them together. The pages of the oldest packets were yellowed and warped, and their edges were uneven rows of ripples.

These were the books of Ember, written over the years by its citizens. They contained in their close-written pages much that was imagined and everything that was known.

Edward Pocket looked up and nodded briefly at Doon, one of his most frequent visitors. Doon nodded back. He went into the fact room, to the section of shelves labelled F. The books were arranged by subject, but even so, it wasn't easy to find what you wanted. A book about moths, for instance, might be under M for moths, or I for insects, or B for bugs. It might even be under F for flying things. Usually you had to browse through the entire library to make sure you'd found all the books on one subject. But since he was looking for fire, he thought he might as well start with F.

Fire was rare in Ember. When there was a fire, it was because there had been an accident – someone had left a dishtowel too close to an electric burner on a stove, or a cord had frayed and a spark had flown out and ignited curtains. Then the citizens would rush in with buckets of water, and the fire was quickly drowned. But it was, of course, possible to start a fire on purpose. You could hold a sliver of wood to the stove burner until it burst into flame, and then for a moment it would flare brightly, giving off orange light.

The trick was to find a way to make the light last.

If you had a light that would keep going, you could go out into the Unknown Regions and see what was there. Finding a way to explore the Unknown Regions was the only thing Doon could think of to do.

He took down a book from the F shelf. *Fungus,* it was called. He put it back. The next book was called *How to Repair Furniture.* He put that back, too. He went through *Foot Diseases, Fun with String, Coping with Failure* and *Canned Fruit Recipes* before he finally found a book called *All About Fire.* He sat down at one of the library's square tables to read it.

But the person who had written the book knew no more about fire than Doon. Mostly the book described the dangers of fire. A long section of it was about a building in Winifred Square that had caught fire forty years ago, and how all its doors and all its furniture had burned up and smoke had filled the air for days. Another part was about what to do if your oven caught on fire.

Doon closed the book and sighed. It was useless. *He* could write a better book than that. He got up and wandered restlessly around the library. Sometimes you could find useful things just by choosing randomly from the shelves. He had done this many times – just reached out and grabbed something – in the hope that by accident he might come upon the very piece of information he needed. It would be something that another person had written down without understanding its significance, just a sentence or two that would be like a flash of light in Doon's mind, fitting together with things he already knew to make a solution to everything.

Although he'd often found something interesting in these searches, he'd never found anything *important*. Today was no different. He did come across a collection called *Mysterious Words from the Past*, which he read for a while. It was about words and phrases so old that their meanings had been forgotten. He read a few pages.

Heavens above
    Indicates surprise. What 'heavens' means
    is unclear. It might be another word for
    'floodlight'.
Hogwash
    Means 'nonsense', though no one knows
    what a 'hog' is or why one would wash
it.
Batting a thousand
    Indicates great success. This might possibly
    refer to killing bugs.
All in the same boat
    Means 'all in the same predicament'.
    The meaning of 'boat' is unknown.

Interesting, but not useful. He put the book back on the shelf and was about to leave when the door of the library opened, and Lina Mayfleet came in.

CHAPTER 9

The Door in the Roped-off Tunnel

Lina saw Doon immediately – he was reaching up to set a book back on its shelf. He saw her, too, when he turned round, and his dark eyebrows flew up in surprise as she hurried over to him.

'Your father told me you were here,' she said. 'Doon, I found something. I want to show it to you.'

'To me? Why?'

'I think it's important. It has to do with the Pipeworks. Will you come to my house and see it?'

'Now?' Doon asked.

Lina nodded.

Doon grabbed his old brown jacket and followed Lina out of the library and across the city to Quillium Square.

Granny's shop was closed and dark when they arrived, and so Lina was surprised when they went upstairs and saw Evaleen Murdo sitting in her place by the window. 'Your grandmother's in her bedroom,'

Mrs Murdo said. 'She didn't feel well, so she asked me to come.'

Poppy was sitting on the floor, banging a spoon on the leg of a chair.

Lina introduced Doon, then led him into the room she shared with Poppy. He looked around, and Lina felt suddenly self-conscious, seeing her room through his eyes. It was a small room with a lot crammed into it. There were two narrow beds, a very small table that fitted into a corner and a four-legged stool to sit on. On the wall, clothes hung from hooks, and more clothes were strewn untidily on the floor. Beneath the window was a brown stain made by the bean seed in its pot on the windowsill. Lina had been watering it every night because she'd promised Clary she would, but it was still nothing but dirt, flat and unpromising.

A couple of shelves beside the window held Lina's important possessions: the pieces of paper she'd collected for drawing, her pencils, a scarf with a silver thread woven through it. On the parts of the wall that had no hooks and no shelves, she had pinned up some of her pictures.

'What are those?' Doon asked.

'They're from my imagination,' Lina said, feeling slightly embarrassed. 'They're pictures of . . . another city.'

'Oh. You made it up.'

'Sort of. Sometimes I dream of it.'

'I draw, too,' said Doon. 'But I draw other kinds of things.'

'Like what?'

'Mostly insects,' said Doon. He told her about his collection of drawings and the worm he was currently observing.

To Lina, this sounded far less interesting than an undiscovered city, but she didn't say so. She led Doon over to the table. 'Here's what I want to show you,' she said. She lifted the metal box. Before she could reach for the papers underneath, Doon took the box and started examining it.

'Where did this come from?' he asked.

'It was in the closet,' Lina said. She told him about Granny's wild search and about finding the box with its lid open and Poppy with paper in her mouth. As she talked, Doon turned the box over in his hands, opened and closed its lid and peered at the latch.

'There's some sort of odd mechanism here,' he said. He tapped at a small metal compartment at the front of the box. 'I'd like to see inside this.'

'Here's what was in the box,' said Lina, lifting the covering paper from her patchwork of scraps. 'At least, it's what's left of what was in there.'

Doon bent over, his hands on either side of the paper.

Lina said, 'It's called "Instructions for Egreston".'

Or maybe "Egresman". Someone's name, anyhow. Maybe a mayor, or a guard. I just call it "The Instructions". I told the mayor about it – I thought maybe it was important. I wrote him a note, but he hasn't answered. I don't think he's interested.'

Doon said nothing.

'You don't have to hold your breath,' said Lina. 'I glued the pieces down. Look,' she said, pointing. 'This word must be *Pipeworks*. And this one *river*. And look at this one – *door*.'

Doon didn't answer. His hair had fallen forward, so Lina couldn't see the expression on his face.

'I thought at first,' Lina went on, 'that it must be instructions for how to do something. How to fix the electricity, maybe. But then I thought, What if it's instructions for going to another place?' Doon said nothing, so Lina went on. 'I mean someplace that isn't here, like another city. I think these instructions say, "Go down into the Pipeworks and look for a door."'

Doon brushed the hair back from his face, but he didn't straighten up. He gazed at the broken words and frowned. 'Edge,' he murmured. 'Small steel pan. What would that mean?'

'A frying pan?' said Lina. 'But I don't know why there'd be a frying pan in the Pipeworks.'

But Doon didn't answer. He seemed to be talking to himself. He kept reading, moving a finger along the lines of words. 'Open,' he whispered. 'Follow.'

Finally he turned to look at Lina. 'I think you're right,' he said. 'I think this *is* important.'

'Oh, I was sure you'd think so!' Lina cried. She was so relieved that her words poured out in a rush. 'Because you take things seriously! You told the truth to the mayor on Assignment Day. I didn't want to believe it, but then came the long blackout, and I knew – I knew things were as bad as you said.' She stopped, breathless. She pointed to a word on the document. 'This door,' she said. 'It has to be a door that leads out of Ember.'

'I don't know,' said Doon. 'Maybe. Or a door that leads to *something* important, even if it isn't that.'

'But it *must* be that – what else could be important enough to lock up in a fancy box?'

'Well . . . I suppose it could be a storage room with some special tools in it or something—' A look of surprise came over his face. 'Actually, I *saw* a door where I didn't expect to see one – out in Tunnel 351. It was locked. I thought it was an old supply closet. I wonder if that could be it.'

'It must be!' cried Lina. Her heart sped up.

'It wasn't anywhere near the river,' Doon said doubtfully.

'That doesn't matter!' Lina said. 'The river goes through the Pipeworks, that's all. It's probably something like, "Go down by the river, then go this way, then that way . . ."'

'Maybe,' said Doon.

'It *must* be!' Lina cried. 'I *know* it is! It's the door that leads out of Ember.'

'I don't know if that makes sense,' said Doon. 'A door in the Pipeworks could only lead to something underground, and how could that . . .'

Lina had no patience for Doon's reasoning. She wanted to dance around the room, she was so excited. 'We have to find out,' she said. 'We have to find out right away!'

Doon looked startled. 'Well, I can go and try the door again,' he said. 'It was locked before, but I suppose . . .'

'I want to go, too,' said Lina.

'You want to come down into the Pipeworks?'

'Yes! Can you get me in?'

Doon thought for a moment. 'I think I can. If you come just at quitting time and wait outside the door, I'll stay out of sight until everyone has gone, and then I'll let you in.'

'Tomorrow?'

'OK. Tomorrow.'

Lina stopped at home the next day only long enough to change out of her messenger jacket, and then she dashed across town to the Pipeworks. Doon met her just outside the door, and she followed him inside, where he handed her a slicker and boots to put on.

They descended the long stone stairway, and when they came out into the main tunnel, Lina stood still, staring at the river. 'I didn't know the river was so big,' she said, after she found her voice.

'Yes,' said Doon. 'Every few years, they say, someone falls in. If you fall in, there's no hope of fishing you out. The river swallows you and sweeps you away.'

Lina shivered. It was cold down here, a cold that she felt all the way through, cold flesh, cold blood, cold bones.

Doon led her up the path beside the water. After a while they came to an opening in the wall, and they turned into it and left the river behind. Doon led the way through winding tunnels. Their rubber boots splashed in pools of water on the floor. Lina thought how awful it would be to work down here all day, every day. It was a creepy place, a place where it seemed people didn't belong. That black river . . . it was like something in a bad dream.

'You have to duck here,' said Doon.

They had come to a roped-off tunnel. 'But there's no light in there,' Lina said.

'No,' said Doon. 'We have to feel our way. It isn't far.' He ducked under the rope and went in, and Lina did the same. They stepped forward into the dark. Lina kept a hand against the damp wall and placed her feet carefully.

'It's right here,' said Doon. He had stopped a few

feet ahead of Lina. She came up behind him. 'Put your hands out,' he said. 'You'll feel it.'

Lina felt a smooth, hard surface. There was a round metal knob, and below the knob, a keyhole. It seemed an ordinary door – not at all like the entrance to a new world. But that was what made things so exciting – nothing was ever how you expected it to be.

'Let's try it,' she whispered.

Doon took hold of the knob and twisted. 'Locked,' he said.

'Is there a pan anywhere?'

'A pan?'

'The instructions said "small steel pan". Maybe that would have the key in it.'

They felt around, but there was nothing – just the rocky walls. They patted the walls, they put their ears to the door, they jiggled the knob and pulled it and pushed it. Finally, Doon said, 'Well, we can't get in. I guess we'd better go.'

And that was when they heard the noise. It was a scuffling, scraping noise that seemed to be coming from somewhere nearby. Lina stopped breathing. She clutched Doon's arm.

'Quick,' Doon whispered. He made his way back towards the lighted tunnel, with Lina following. They ducked under the rope and rounded a turn, then stopped, stood still and listened. A harsh scraping sound. A thud. A pause . . . and then the sound of an impact, a short, explosive breath and a muttered word in a gruff, low voice.

Then slow footsteps, getting closer.

They flattened themselves against the wall and stood motionless. The footsteps stopped briefly, and there was another grunt. Then the steps continued, but seemed to be fading. In a moment, from a distance, there was another sound: the chink of a key turning in a lock, and the click of a latch opening.

Lina made an astonished face at Doon. Someone had gone down the roped tunnel and opened the door! She put her mouth close to Doon's ear. 'Shall we try to see who it is?' she whispered.

Doon shook his head. 'I don't think we should,' he said. 'We should go.'

'We could just peek round the corner.'

It was too tempting not to try. They crept forwards to the place where the tunnel turned. From there they could see the entrance to the roped tunnel. Holding their breath, they watched.

And in a minute, they heard a thump and click – the door closing, the lock turning – and footsteps once again, this time quick. A long leg stepped over the rope, and the person it belonged to turned and walked away. All they saw was his back – a dark coat, dark untidy hair. He walked with a lurching motion that struck Lina as somehow familiar. In a few seconds, he had vanished into the shadows.

* * *

When they came up out of the Pipeworks, they stripped off their boots and slickers and hurried out into Plummer Square, where they flopped down on a bench and burst into furious talk.

'Someone got there before us!' said Lina.

Doon said, 'He was walking slowly when he went in – as if he was looking for something. And he walked fast when he came out . . .'

'As if he'd *found* something! What *was* it? I can't stand not to know!'

Doon jumped up. He paced back and forth in front of the bench.

'But how did he get the key?' he asked. 'Did he find Instructions like the ones you found? And how did he get into the Pipeworks? I don't think he works there.'

'There's something familiar about the way he walks,' said Lina. 'But I don't know why.'

'Well, anyhow, he opened that door and we can't,' said Doon. 'If it *does* go somewhere, if it *does* lead out of Ember, he'll be telling the whole city pretty soon. He'll be a hero.' Doon sat down again. 'If he's found the way out, we'll be glad, of course,' he said glumly. 'It doesn't matter who finds it, as long as it helps the city.'

'That's right,' Lina said.

'It's just that I thought *we* were going to find it,'

said Doon.

'Yes,' Lina said, thinking how grand it would have been to stand before all of Ember, announcing their discovery.

They sat without talking for a while, lost in their own thoughts. A man pulling a cart full of wood scraps went by. A woman leaned from a lighted window on Gappery Street and called out to some boys playing in the square below. A couple of guards, in their red and brown uniforms, ambled across the square, laughing. The town clock rang out six deep booms that Lina could feel, like shudders, beneath her ribs.

Doon said, 'I guess what we do now is wait to see if there's an announcement.'

'I guess so,' said Lina.

'Maybe that door is nothing special after all,' said Doon. 'Maybe it's just an old unused supply closet.'

But Lina wasn't ready to believe that. Maybe it wasn't the door out of Ember, but it was a mystery nevertheless – a mystery connected, she was sure, to the bigger mystery they were trying to solve.

CHAPTER 10

Blue Sky and Goodbye

Lina slept restlessly that night. She had frightening dreams in which something dangerous was lurking in the darkness. When the lights went on in the morning and she opened her eyes, her first thought was of the door in the Pipeworks – and then right away she felt a thud of disappointment, because the door was locked and someone else, not her, knew what was behind it.

She went in to wake Granny. 'Time to get up,' she said, but Granny didn't answer. She was lying with her mouth half open and breathing in a strange hoarse way. 'Don't feel too good,' she finally said in a weak voice.

Lina felt Granny's forehead. It was hot. Her hands were very cold. She ran for Mrs Murdo and after that to Cloving Square to tell Captain Fleery she would not be coming to work today. Then she ran to Oliver Street, to the office of Dr Tower, where she banged on the door until the doctor opened it.

Dr Tower was a thin woman with uncombed hair and shadows under her eyes. When she saw Lina, she seemed to grow even more tired.

'Dr Tower,' Lina said, 'my grandmother is sick. Will you come?'

'I will,' she said. 'But I can't promise to help her. I'm low on medicine.'

'But come and look. Maybe she doesn't need medicine.'

Lina led the doctor the few blocks to her house. When she saw Granny, the doctor sighed. 'How are you, Granny Mayfleet?' she asked.

Granny looked at the doctor blearily. 'I think ill,' she said.

Dr Tower laid a hand across her forehead. She asked her to stick out her tongue, and she listened to her heart and her breathing.

'She has a fever,' the doctor told Lina. 'You'll need to stay home with her today. Make her some soup. Give her water to drink. Put rags in cool water and lay them across her forehead.' She picked up Granny's bony hand in her rough, reddish one. 'What's best for you is to sleep today,' she said. 'Your good granddaughter will take care of you.'

And all day, that's what Lina did. She made a thin soup of spinach and onions and fed it to Granny a spoonful at a time. She stroked Granny's forehead, held her hand and talked to her about cheerful things.

133

She kept Poppy as quiet as she could. But as she did all this, in the back of her mind was the memory of the days of her father's illness, when he seemed to grow dim like a lamp losing power, and the sound of his breathing was like water gurgling through a clogged pipe. Though she didn't want to, she also remembered the evening when her father let out one last short breath and didn't take another, and the morning a few months later when Dr Tower emerged from her mother's bedroom with a crying baby and a face that was heavy with bad news.

In the late afternoon, Granny got restless. She lifted herself up on one elbow. 'Did we find it?' she asked Lina. 'Did we ever find it?'

'Find what, Granny?'

'The thing that was lost,' Granny said. 'The old thing that my grandfather lost . . .'

'Yes,' said Lina. 'Don't worry, Granny, we found it, it's safe now.'

'Oh, good.' Granny sank back onto her pillows and smiled at the ceiling. 'What a relief,' she said. She coughed a couple of times, closed her eyes and fell asleep.

Lina stayed home from work the next day as well. It was a long day. Granny dozed most of the time. Poppy, delighted to have Lina at home to play with, kept toddling over with things she found – dust rags, kitchen spoons, stray shoes – and whacking them against Lina's knees, saying, 'Play wif dis! Play wif dis!' Lina was glad to play with her, but after a while she'd had enough of spoon-banging and rag-tugging and shoe-rolling. 'Let's do something else,' she said to Poppy. 'Shall we draw?'

Granny had drunk a full cup of soup for dinner and was falling asleep again, so Lina got out her coloured pencils and two of the can labels she'd been saving – they were white on the back and made good enough drawing paper, if you flattened them out. With their sharpest kitchen knife, she whittled the pencils into points. She gave the green pencil and one can label to Poppy, and she herself took the blue pencil and smoothed out the other can label on the table.

What would she draw? Taking hold of a pencil was like opening a tap inside her mind through which her imagination flowed. She could feel the pictures ready to come out. It was a sort of pressure, like water in a pipe. She always thought she would draw something wonderful, but what she actually drew never quite matched the feeling. It was like when she tried to tell a dream – the words never really captured how it felt.

Poppy was grasping the pencil in her fist and making a wild scribble. 'Lookit!' she cried.

'Lovely,' said Lina. Then, without even a clear idea of what it was to be, she began her own picture. She started on the left side of the can label. First she drew a tall, narrow box – a building. Then more boxes next to it – a cluster of buildings. Next she drew a few tiny people walking on the street below the buildings. It was what she nearly always drew – the other city – and every time she drew it, she had the same frustrating feeling: there was more to be drawn. There were other things in this city, there were marvels there – but she couldn't imagine what they were. All she knew was that this city was bright in a different way from Ember. Where the brightness came from she didn't know.

She drew more buildings and filled in the windows and doors; she put in streetlamps; she added a greenhouse. All the way across the paper, she drew buildings of different sizes. All the buildings were white, because that was the colour of the paper.

She set her pencil down for a moment and studied what she'd done. It was time to fill in the sky. In the pictures she'd done with regular pencils, the sky was its true colour, black. But this time she made it blue, since she was using her blue pencil. Methodically, as Poppy scratched and scribbled beside her, Lina coloured in the space above the buildings, her pencil moving back and forth in short lines, until the entire sky was blue.

She sat back and looked at her picture. Wouldn't it be strange, she thought, to have a blue sky? But she liked the way it looked. It would be beautiful – a blue sky.

Poppy had started using her pencil to poke holes in her paper. Lina folded up her own picture and took Poppy's away from her. 'Time for dinner,' she said.

Sometime deep in the night, Lina woke suddenly, thinking she'd heard something. Had she been dreaming? She lay still, her eyes open in the darkness. The sound came again, a weak, trembling call: 'Lina . . .'

She got up and started for Granny's room. Though she had lived in the same house all her life, she still had trouble finding her way at night, when the darkness was complete. It was as if walls had shifted slightly, and furniture moved to new places. Lina stayed close to the walls, feeling her way along. Here was her bedroom door. Here was the kitchen and the table – she winced as she stubbed her toe on one of its legs. A little farther and she'd come to the far wall and the door to Granny's room. Granny's voice was like a thin line in the dark air. 'Lina . . . Come and help . . . I need . . .'

'I'm coming, Granny,' she called.

She stumbled over something – a shoe, maybe – and fell against the bed. 'Here I am, Granny!' she said. She felt for Granny's hand – it was very cold.

'I feel so strange,' said Granny. Her voice was a whisper. 'I dreamed . . . I dreamed about my baby . . . or someone's baby . . .'

Lina sat down on the bed. Carefully she moved her hands over the narrow ridge of her grandmother's body until she came to her shoulders. There her fingers tangled in the long wisps of Granny's hair. She pressed a finger against the side of Granny's throat to feel for her pulse, as the doctor had shown her. It was fluttery, like a moth that has hurt itself and is flapping in crooked circles.

'Can I get you some water, Granny?' Lina asked. She couldn't think what else to do.

'No water,' Granny said. 'Just stay for a while.'

Lina tucked one foot underneath her and pulled part of the blanket over her lap. She took hold of Granny's hand again and stroked it gently with one finger.

For a long time neither of them said anything. Lina sat listening to her grandmother's breathing. She would take a deep, shuddering breath and let it out in a sigh. Then there would be a long silence before the next breath began. Lina closed her eyes. No use keeping them open – there was nothing to see but the dark. She was aware only of her grandmother's cold, thin hand and the sound of her breathing. Every now and then Granny would mumble a few words Lina couldn't make out, and then Lina would stroke her forehead and say, 'Don't worry, it's all right. It's almost morning,' though she didn't know if it was or not.

After a long time, Granny stirred slightly and

seemed to come awake. 'You go to bed, dear,' she said. 'I'm all right now.' Her voice was clear but very faint. 'You go back to sleep.'

Lina bent forward until her head rested against Granny's shoulder. Granny's soft hair tickled her face. 'All right, then,' she whispered. 'Good night, Granny.' She squeezed her grandmother's shoulders gently, and as she stood up a wave of terrible loneliness swept over her. She wanted to see Granny's face. But the darkness hid everything. It might still be a long time until morning – she didn't know. She groped her way back to her own bed and fell into a deep sleep, and when, hours later, the clock tower struck six and the lights came on, Lina went fearfully into her grandmother's room. She found her very pale and very still, all the life gone out of her.

CHAPTER 11

Lizzie's Groceries

Lina spent all that day in Mrs Murdo's house, which was just like theirs only neater. There was one couch, and one fat chair covered in fuzzy striped material, and one big table, only Mrs Murdo's table wasn't wobbly like theirs. On the table was a basket, and in the basket were three turnips, each of them lavender on one end and white on the other. Mrs Murdo must have put them there, Lina thought, not just because she was going to have them for dinner, but also because they were beautiful.

Lina sat sideways on the couch with her legs stretched out, and Mrs Murdo covered her with a soft grey-green blanket. 'This will keep you warm,' she said, tucking it around Lina's legs. Lina didn't really feel cold but she did feel sad, which was in a way the same. The blanket felt good, like someone holding her. Mrs Murdo gave Poppy a long purple scarf to play with and made a creamy mushroom soup with potatoes, and all day Lina stayed there, snuggled under the blanket. She thought about her grandmother, who had had a long and mostly cheerful life. She cried some and fell asleep. She woke up and played with Poppy. The day had a strange but comforting feel to it, like a rest between the end of one time and the beginning of another.

On the morning of the next day, Lina got up and got ready to go to work. Mrs Murdo gave her beet tea and spinach hash for breakfast. 'The Singing's coming up soon,' she remarked to Lina as they ate. 'Do you know your part?'

'Yes,' said Lina. 'I remember it pretty well from last year.'

'I rather like the Singing,' said Mrs Murdo.

'I love it,' Lina said. 'I think it's my favourite day of the year.' Once a year, the people of the city came together to sing the three great songs of Ember. Just thinking of it made Lina feel better. She finished her breakfast and put on her red jacket.

'Don't worry about Poppy, I'll take care of her,' said Mrs Murdo as Lina headed for the door. 'When you come back this evening, we'll talk about how to proceed.'

'Proceed?' said Lina.

'Well, you can't live by yourselves, just the two of you, can you?'

'We can't?'

'Certainly not,' said Mrs Murdo sternly. 'Who's to take care of Poppy while you go off delivering messages? You must move in here with me. I have an empty bedroom, after all, and quite a nice one. Come and look.'

She opened a door at the far end of the living room, and Lina peeked in. She had never seen such a beautiful cosy room. There was a big lumpy bed covered with a faded blue blanket, and at its head four plump pillows. Next to the bed was a chest of drawers with drawer handles shaped like teardrops and a mirror attached to the top. The carpets on the floor were all different shades of blue and green, and in the corner was a sturdy square table and a chair with a back like a ladder. 'This will be your room,' said Mrs Murdo. 'Yours and Poppy's. You'll have to share the bed, but it's big enough.'

'It's lovely,' Lina said. 'You're so kind, Mrs Murdo.'

'Well,' said Mrs Murdo briskly, 'it's just common sense. You need a place. I have one. You go on now, and I'll see you this evening.'

Three days had passed since Lina and Doon had seen the man in the Pipeworks, and there hadn't been any special announcements. So if that man had discovered a way out of Ember, he was keeping the news to himself. Lina couldn't understand why.

As Lina ran through the city with her messages

on her first day back to work, it seemed to her that the mood of the people was even gloomier than before. There were long, silent lines at the markets, and knots of people gathered in the squares, talking in low voices. Many shops – more each day, it seemed – displayed signs in their windows saying 'Closed' or 'Open Mon. Tues. Only'. Every now and then, the lights flickered, and people stopped and looked up in fright. When the flickering ended, and the lights stayed lit, people just took a breath and walked on.

Lina delivered her messages as usual, but inside she felt strange. Everywhere she ran, she heard the same words, like a drumbeat, in her mind: *alone in the world, alone in the world.* It wasn't exactly true. She had Poppy. She had friends. And she had Mrs Murdo, who was somewhere between a friend and a relative. But she felt as if she had suddenly got older in the last three days. She was a sort of mother herself now. What happened to Poppy was more or less up to her.

As the day went on, she stopped thinking *alone in the world* and began thinking about her new life at Mrs Murdo's. She thought about the blue-green room and planned how she would arrange her pictures on the walls. The one she'd drawn with her blue pencil would look especially nice, because it would match the colour of the rugs. She could bring her pillows from home and add them to the ones on the bed, and then she'd have six altogether – and maybe she could find some old blue dresses or shirts and make pillow covers for them. The blue-green room, the orderly apartment, the meals cooked and the blankets tucked in cosily at night – all this gave her a feeling of comfort, almost luxury. She was grateful for Mrs Murdo's kindness. I am not ready yet to be alone in the world, she thought.

Late that afternoon, Lina was given a message to take to Lampling Street. She delivered the message and, as she was coming back out onto the street, caught sight of Lizzie coming out the door of the Supply Depot – her orange hair was unmistakable. 'Lizzie!' Lina called out.

Lizzie must not have heard her. She kept on going. Lina called again. 'Lizzie, wait!' This time it was clear that Lizzie had heard, but instead of stopping, she walked faster. What's the matter with her? Lina wondered. She ran after her and grabbed the back of her coat. 'Lizzie, it's me!'

Lizzie stopped and turned round. 'Oh!' she said. Her face was flushed. 'It's you. Hi! I thought it was . . . I didn't realize it was you.' She smiled brightly, but there was a distracted look in her eyes. 'I was just going home,' she said. Her arms were wrapped around a small bulging sack.

'I'll walk with you,' said Lina.

'Oh,' said Lizzie. 'Oh, good.' But she didn't look pleased.

'Lizzie, something sad has happened,' Lina said. 'My grandmother died.'

Lizzie gave her a quick sideways glance, but she didn't stop walking. 'That's too bad,' she said absently. 'Poor you.'

What was wrong with her? Lizzie was ordinarily so interested in other people's misfortunes. She could be sincerely sympathetic, too, when she wasn't wrapped up in her own troubles.

Lina changed the subject. 'What's in the sack?' she asked.

'Oh, just some groceries,' said Lizzie. 'I stopped at the market after work.'

'You did?' Lina was confused. She had seen Lizzie not two minutes ago leaving the storeroom office.

Lizzie didn't answer. She began walking and talking quite fast. 'It was so busy today at work. Work is so hard, isn't it, Lina? I think work is much harder than school, and not as interesting. You do the same thing every day. I get so *tired,* don't you, running around all day?'

Lina started to say that she liked running and hardly ever got tired, but Lizzie didn't wait for her to answer.

'Oh, well, at least there are some good things about it. Guess what, Lina? I have a boyfriend. I met him at work. He really likes me – he says my hair is the exact colour of a red-hot burner on a stove.'

Lina laughed. 'It's true, Lizzie,' she said. 'You look like your head is on fire.'

Lizzie laughed, too, and lifted one hand to fluff her hair. She puckered her lips and fluttered her eyelashes. 'He says I'm as beautiful as a red tomato.'

They were crossing Torrick Square now. It was crowded in the square. People had just left work and were lining up at the shops and hurrying along with packages. A cluster of children sat on the pavement, playing some sort of game.

'Who is this boyfriend?' asked Lina.

But just at that moment, Lizzie tripped. She'd been strutting along being beautiful, not paying attention to her feet, and the edge of her shoe caught on an uneven place in the pavement. She staggered and fell, and as she fell she lost her grip on the sack. It hit the ground and toppled sideways, and some cans spilled out. They rolled in all different directions.

Lina reached for Lizzie's arm. 'Did you hurt yourself?' she asked, but Lizzie went scrambling after the cans so quickly it was clear she wasn't hurt. Wanting to help, Lina went after the cans, too. Two had rolled under a bench. Another was going towards the children, who were on their feet now, watching Lizzie's wild spider-like motions. Lina picked up the cans under the bench, and for a second her breath stopped. One of them was a can of peaches. 'Peaches', it said right on it, and there was a picture of a yellow globe.

No one she knew had seen a can of peaches in years. She looked at the other one. It was just as amazing – 'Creamed Corn', it said. Lina remembered having creamed corn once, as a thrilling treat, when she was five years old.

There was a shout. She looked up. One of the children had picked up a can. 'Look at this!' he cried, and the other children gathered around him. 'Apple sauce!' he said, and the children murmured, 'Apple sauce, apple sauce,' as if they had never heard the word before.

Lizzie was on her feet. She had all the cans except for the two in Lina's hands and the one the child had picked up. She stood there for a moment, her eyes flicking back and forth from Lina to the children. Then she smiled, a bright fake-looking smile. 'Thanks for helping me,' she said. 'I found these on a back shelf at the market. What a surprise, huh? You can keep those.' She waved the back of her hand at the children, waved again at Lina, and then took off, holding the sack by its neck so it hung beside her and banged against her legs.

Lina didn't follow her. She walked home, thinking about Lizzie's sack of cans. You simply did not find cans of peaches and apple sauce and creamed corn on the back shelves of markets. Lizzie was lying. And if the cans hadn't come from a market, where had they come from? There was only one answer: they had come from the storerooms. Somehow, Lizzie had got them because she worked in the storeroom office. Had she paid for them? How much? Or had she taken them without paying?

Mrs Murdo had cooked a dinner of beet-and-bean stew for them that night. When Lina showed her the two cans, she gasped in astonishment. 'Where did you get these?' she asked.

'From a friend,' said Lina.

'And where did your friend get them?'

Lina shrugged. 'I don't know.'

Mrs Murdo frowned slightly but didn't ask any more questions. She opened the cans, and they had a feast: creamed corn with their stew, and peaches for dessert. It was the best meal Lina had had in a very long time – but her enjoyment of it was tainted just a little by the question of where it had come from.

The next morning, Lina headed for Broad Street. Before she started delivering messages today, she was going to have a talk with Lizzie.

She spied her half a block from the storeroom office. She was sauntering along looking in shop windows. A long green scarf was wound around her neck.

Lina ran up swiftly behind her. 'Lizzie,' she said.

Lizzie whirled round. When she saw Lina, she flinched. She didn't say anything, just turned round and kept walking.

Lina caught hold of one end of the green scarf and jerked Lizzie to a halt. 'Lizzie!' she said. 'Stop!'

'What for?' Lizzie said. 'I'm going to work.' She tried to pull away, but she didn't get far, because Lina had a firm grip on her scarf.

Lina spoke in a low voice. There were people all around them – a couple of old men leaning against the wall, a group of chattering children just ahead, workers going toward the storerooms – and she didn't want to be overheard. 'You have to tell me where you got those cans,' she said.

'I told you. I found them on a back shelf at the market. Let go of my scarf.' Lizzie tried to wrench her scarf out of Lina's grip, but Lina held on.

'You didn't,' Lina said. 'No market would just forget about things like that. Tell me the truth.' She gave a yank on the end of the scarf.

'Stop it!' Lizzie reached out and grabbed a handful of Lina's hair. Lina yelped and pulled harder on the scarf, and the two of them scuffled, snatching at each other's hair and coats. They knocked against a woman who snapped at them angrily, and finally they toppled over, sitting down hard on the pavement.

Lina was the first one to laugh. It was so much like what they used to do in fun, chasing each other and screaming with laughter. Now here they were again, nearly grown girls, sitting in a heap on the pavement.

After a moment, Lizzie laughed, too. 'You dope,' she said. 'All right, I'll tell you. I sort of wanted to anyway.' Lizzie leaned forward with her elbows on her knees and lowered her voice. 'Well, it's this,' she said. 'There's a storeroom worker named Looper. He's a carrier. Do you know him? He was two classes ahead of us. Looper Windly.'

'I know who he is,' said Lina. 'I took a message for him on my first day of work. Tall, with a long skinny neck. Big teeth. Funny-looking.'

Lizzie looked hurt. 'Well, I wouldn't describe him *that* way. I think he's handsome.'

Lina shrugged. 'OK. Go on.'

'Looper explores the storerooms. He goes into every room that isn't locked. He wants to know the *true situation,* Lina. He's not like most workers, who just plod along doing their jobs and then go home. He wants to find things out.'

'And what has he found out?' Lina asked.

'He's found out that there's still a little bit left of some rare things, just a few things in rooms here and there that have been forgotten. You know, Lina,' she said, 'there are *so many* rooms down there. Some of them, way out at the edges, are marked "Empty" in the ledger book, and so no one ever goes there any more. But Looper found out that they're not all empty.'

'So he's been taking things.'

'Just a few things! And not often.'

'And he's giving some to you.'

'Yes. Because he likes me.' Lizzie smiled a little smile and hugged her arms together. I see, Lina thought. She feels *that* way about Looper.

'But Looper's stealing,' said Lina. 'And Lizzie – he isn't just stealing things for you. He has a store! He steals things and sells them for huge prices!'

'He does not,' said Lizzie, but she looked worried.

'He does. I know because I bought something from him just a few weeks ago. He has a whole box of coloured pencils.'

Lizzie scowled. 'He never gave me any coloured pencils.'

'He shouldn't be giving you anything – or selling things. Don't you think everyone should know about this food he found?'

'No!' Lizzie cried. 'Listen. If there's only one can of peaches left, only one person gets to have it, right? So why should everyone know? They'd just end up fighting over it. What good would that be?' Lizzie reached out and put a hand on Lina's knee. 'Listen,' she said. 'I'll ask Looper to find some good stuff for you, too. I know he will, if I ask him.'

Before she had time to think, Lina heard herself saying, 'What kind of good stuff?'

Lizzie's eyes gleamed. 'There's two packages of coloured paper, he told me. And some cough medicine. And there's three pairs of girls' shoes.'

It was treasure. Coloured paper! And cough medicine to cure sickness, and shoes . . . she hadn't had new ones for almost two years. Lina's heart raced. What Lizzie said was true: if everyone knew there were still a few wonderful things in the storerooms, people would fight each other trying to get them. But what if no one knew? What difference would it make if she had the coloured paper, or the shoes? She suddenly wanted those things so badly she felt weak. A picture arose in her mind's eye – the shelves at Mrs Murdo's house stocked with good things, and the three of them happier and safer than other people.

Lizzie leaned closer and lowered her voice. 'Looper found a can of pineapple. I was going to split it with him, but I'll give you a bite if you promise not to tell.'

Pineapple! That delectable long-lost thing that her grandmother had told her about. Was there anything wrong with having a bite of it, just to see what it was like?

'I've already tasted peaches, apple sauce and a thing called fruit cocktail,' said Lizzie. 'And prunes and creamed corn and cranberry sauce and asparagus . . .'

'All *that*?' Lina was astonished. 'Then there's a lot of special things like that still?'

'No,' said Lizzie. 'Not a lot at all. In fact, we've finished all those.'

'You and Looper?'

Lizzie nodded, smiling smugly. 'Looper says it's all going to be gone soon anyway, why not live as well as we can right now?'

'But Lizzie, why should *you* get all that? Why you and not other people?'

'Because we found it. Because we can get at it.'

'I don't think it's fair,' said Lina.

Lizzie spoke as if she were talking to a not-very-bright child. 'You can have some, *too*. That's what I'm *telling* you. There are still a few good things left.'

But that wasn't the unfairness Lina was thinking of. It was that just two people were getting things that everyone would have wanted. She couldn't think how it should have been done. You couldn't divide a can of apple sauce evenly among all the people in the city. Still, something was wrong with grabbing the good things just because you *could*. It seemed not only unfair to everyone else but bad for the person who was doing it, somehow. She remembered the hunger she'd felt when Looper showed her the coloured pencils. It wasn't a pleasant feeling. She didn't *want* to want things that way.

She stood up. 'I don't want anything from Looper.'

Lizzie shrugged. 'OK,' she said, but there was a

look of dismay on her small pale face. 'Too bad for you.'

'Thanks anyway,' said Lina, and she set off across Torrick Square, walking fast at first and then breaking into a run.

CHAPTER 12

A Dreadful Discovery

About a week after he and Lina had seen the man come out of the mysterious door, Doon was assigned to fix a clog in Tunnel 207. It turned out to be easy. He undid the pipe, rammed a long thin brush down it, and a jet of water spurted into his face. Once he'd put the pipe back together, he had nothing else to do. So he decided to go out to Tunnel 351 and take another look at the locked door. It was strange, he thought, that no announcement about a way out of Ember had come. Maybe that door had not been what they thought it was.

So he set out for the south end of the Pipeworks. When he came to the roped-off passage in Tunnel 351, he ducked in and walked along through the dark, feeling his way. He was pretty sure the door would be locked as usual. His mind was on other things. He was thinking of his green worm, which had been behaving oddly, refusing to eat and hanging from the side of its box with its chin tucked in. And he was thinking about Lina, whom he hadn't seen for several days. He wondered where she was. When he came to the door, he reached absently for the knob, and what he felt startled him so much that he snatched his hand back as if he'd been stung. He felt again, carefully. There was a *key* in the lock!

For a long moment, Doon stood as still as a statue. Then he took hold of the doorknob and turned it. Very slowly, he pushed on the door. It swung inward without a sound.

He opened it only a few inches, just enough to peer around the edge. What he saw made him gasp.

There was no road, or passage, or stairway behind the door. There was a brightly lit room, whose size he could not guess at because it was so crowded with things. On all sides were crates and boxes, sacks and bundles and packages. There were mounds of cans, heaps of clothes, rows of jars and bottles, stacks of light-bulb packages. Piles rose to the low ceiling and leaned against the walls, blocking all but a small space in the centre. In that small space, a little living room had been set up. There was a greenish rug, and on the rug an armchair and a table. On the table were dishes smeared with the remains of food, and in the armchair facing Doon was a great blob of a person whose head was flopped backwards, so that all Doon could see of it was an upthrust chin. The blob stirred and muttered, and Doon, in the second before he stepped back and pulled the door closed, caught a glimpse of a fleshy ear, a slab of grey cheek and a loose, purplish mouth.

That day, Lina had more messages to carry than ever. There had been five blackouts in a row during the week. They were all fairly short – the longest was four and a half minutes, Lina had heard – but there had never been so many so close together. Everyone was nervous. People who might ordinarily walk to some-one's house were sending messages instead. Often they didn't even come out into the street but beck-oned to a messenger from their doorway.

By five o'clock, Lina had carried thirty-nine messages. Most of them were more or less the same: 'I'm not coming to the meeting tonight, decided to stay home.' 'I won't be in to work tomorrow.' 'Instead of meeting me in Cloving Square, why don't you come to my house?' The citizens of Ember were hun-kering down, burrowing in. Fewer people stood around talking in groups under the lights in the squares. Instead, they would pause briefly to murmur a few words to each other and then hasten onward.

Lina was on her way home to Mrs Murdo's – she and Poppy had moved in with all their things – when she heard rapid footsteps. Startled, she turned and saw Doon racing towards her.

At first he was so out of breath he couldn't speak.

'What is it? What *is* it?' said Lina.

'The door,' he panted. 'The door in 351. I opened it.'

Lina's heart leaped. 'You did?'

Doon nodded.

'Is it the way out?' Lina whispered fiercely.

'No,' Doon said. He glanced behind him. Clutching Lina's arm, he pulled her into a shadowy spot on the street. 'It doesn't lead out of Ember,' he whispered. 'It leads to a big room.'

Lina's face fell. 'A room? What's in there?'

'Everything. Food, clothes, boxes, cans. Light bulbs, stacks of them. Everything. Piles and piles up to the ceiling.' His eyes grew wide. 'And someone was there, in the middle of it all, asleep.'

'Who?'

A look of horror passed over Doon's face. 'The mayor,' he said. 'Conked out in a big armchair, with an empty plate in front of him.'

'The mayor!' Lina whispered.

'Yes. The mayor has a secret treasure room in the Pipeworks.'

They stared at each other, speechless. Then Doon suddenly stamped hard on the pavement. His face flushed red. '*That's* the solution he keeps telling us about. It's a solution for *him*, not the rest of us. He gets everything he needs, and we get the leftovers! He doesn't care about the city. All he cares about is his fat stomach!'

Lina felt dizzy, as if she'd been hit on the head. 'What will we do?' She couldn't think, she was so stunned.

'Tell everyone!' said Doon. He was shaking with anger. 'Tell the whole city the mayor is robbing us!'

'Wait, wait.' Lina put a hand on Doon's arm and concentrated for a minute. 'Come on,' she said at last. 'Let's go sit in Harken Square. I have something to tell you, too.'

At the north end of Harken Square stood a circle of Believers, clapping their hands and singing one of their songs. Lately they seemed to be singing more loudly and cheerfully than ever. Their voices were shrill. 'Coming soon to save us!' they wailed. 'Happy, happy day!'

Near the Gathering Hall steps, something un-usual was happening. Twenty or so people were pac-ing round and round, carrying big signs painted on old planks and on big banners made of sheets. The signs said 'WHAT solutions, Mayor Cole?' and 'We want ANSWERS!' Every now and then the demon-strators would yell these slogans out loud. Lina won-dered if the mayor was paying any attention.

Doon and Lina found an empty bench on the south side of Harken Square and sat down.

'Now, listen,' said Lina.

'I *am* listening,' said Doon, though his face was still red and the look on his face was stormy.

'I saw Lizzie coming out of the storerooms yesterday,' Lina said. She told him about the cans, and Lizzie's new friend, Looper, and what Looper was doing.

Doon pounded his fist on his leg. 'That's *two* of them doing it, then,' he said.

'Wait, there's more. Remember how I thought there was something familiar about the man who came out the door? I've remembered what. It was that way he walked, sort of dipping over sideways, and also that hair, that black hair all unbrushed and sticking out. I've seen him twice. I don't know why I didn't remember who it was right away – maybe because I've only seen him from the front. I took a message for him on my first day.'

Doon was jiggling with impatience. 'Well, who was it, *who was it*?'

'It was Looper. Looper, who works in the storerooms. Lizzie's boyfriend. And Doon,' Lina leaned forward. 'It was a message to the *mayor* that he gave me, and it was this: 'Delivery at eight''.

Doon's mouth dropped open. 'So that means . . .'

'He's taking things from the storeroom for the mayor. And he's giving some to Lizzie, and selling some in his store.'

'Oh!' cried Doon. He slapped his hand against his head. 'Why didn't I get it before? There's a hatch in the ceiling near Tunnel 351. It must go right up into the storerooms. Looper comes through there! *That's* what we heard that day, remember? A sort of scraping – that would have been the hatch opening. Then a thud – his sack of stuff dropping through – and then a sound like someone jumping down and landing hard on the ground.'

'And then walking slowly—'

'Because he was carrying a load!'

'And walking quickly on the way out because he'd left it all for the mayor.' Lina took a deep breath. Her heart was drumming and her hands were cold. 'We have to think what to do,' she said. 'If this were an ordinary situation, the mayor would be the one to tell.'

'But the mayor is the one committing the crime,' said Doon.

'So then we should tell the guards, I guess,' said Lina. 'They're next in authority to the mayor. Though I don't like them much,' she added, remembering how she'd been so roughly hustled down the stairs from the roof of the Gathering Hall. 'Especially the chief guard.'

'But you're right,' Doon said. 'We should tell the guards. They'll go down into the Pipeworks and see for themselves that we're telling the truth. Then they can arrest the mayor and have all the stuff put back in the storerooms, and *then* they can tell the city what's been going on.'

'That's a much better idea,' said Lina. 'Then you and I can get back to what's more important.'

'What?'

'Figuring out the Instructions. Now that we know that the door we found wasn't the right one, we have to *find* the right one.'

'I don't know,' said Doon. 'We might be all wrong about those Instructions. They could just be about some old Pipeworks tool closet.' He made a sour face. '*Instructions for Egreston*. Who's Egreston? Or Egresman? Or whoever it was? Why couldn't he have been just an especially stupid Pipeworks guy who needed instructions to find his way around?' He shook his head. 'I don't know. I think maybe those Instructions are just hogwash.'

'Hogwash? What's that?'

'It means nonsense. I read it in a book in the library.'

'But they can't be nonsense! Why would they have been kept in a box like that? With the strange lock?'

But Doon didn't want to think about the Instructions right then. 'We'll figure it out tomorrow,' he said. 'Right now, let's go find the guards.'

'Wait,' said Lina, catching hold of the sleeve of his

jacket. 'I have one more thing to tell you.'

'What?'

'My grandmother died.'

'Oh!' Doon's face fell. 'That's so sad,' he said. 'I'm sorry.' His sympathy made tears spring to Lina's eyes. Doon looked startled for a moment, and then he took a step towards her and wrapped his arms around her. He gave her a squeeze so quick and tight that it made her cough, and then it made her laugh. She realized all at once that Doon – thin, dark-eyed Doon with his troublesome temper and his terrible brown jacket and his good heart – was the person that she knew better than anyone now. He was her best friend.

'Thanks,' she said. 'Well.' She smiled at him. 'Let's go and talk to the guard.'

They crossed the square and climbed the steps of the Gathering Hall. Sitting at the big reception desk outside the door of the mayor's office was the assistant guard, Barton Snode, the same one Lina had encountered her first time here. Snode looked bored. His elbows were on the desk, and his chin was moving very slowly from side to side.

'Sir,' said Doon, 'we need to speak with you.'

The guard looked up. 'Certainly,' he said. 'Go right ahead.'

'In private,' said Lina.

The guard looked puzzled. His small eyes darted

back and forth. 'This is private,' he said. 'No one here but me.'

'But anyone could come along,' said Doon. 'What we have to say is secret, and very important.'

'Very important?' said Snode. 'Secret?' His face brightened. Grunting, he raised himself up from his chair and motioned them into a narrow hallway off to the side of the main hall. 'What is it?' he said.

They told him. As they spoke, interrupting each other to make sure they got in all the details, the guard's eyebrows gradually lifted higher and higher over his eyes. 'You *saw* this room?' he said. 'This is true? Are you sure?' He was chewing faster now. 'You mean the mayor . . . you mean the mayor is . . .'

At that moment, a little way down the hall, a door opened. Through it came three more guards, including – Lina spotted him by his beard – the chief guard. They strode forward, talking to each other in low voices, and as they passed, the chief guard threw a quick glance at Lina. Does he recognize me? Lina wondered. She couldn't tell.

Barton Snode finished his sentence in a husky whisper. 'You mean . . . the mayor is *stealing*?'

'That's right,' said Doon. 'We thought you should be informed, because who else can arrest the mayor? And once you've done that, the guards can put all the things he's stolen back where they came from.'

'And then tell the city that a new mayor has to be

found,' added Lina.

Barton Snode leaned heavily against the wall and rubbed a hand over his chin. He seemed to be thinking. 'Something must be done,' he said. 'This is shocking, shocking.' He started back towards his desk, and Doon and Lina followed. 'I will make a note,' he said, taking a pencil from the desk drawer. Lina watched as he wrote slowly on a scrap of paper: 'Mayor stealing. Secret room.'

When he'd finished, he let out a satisfied breath. 'Very good,' he said. 'Action will be taken, you may be sure. Some sort of action. Quite soon.'

'Good,' said Doon.

'Thank you,' said Lina, and they turned to leave.

The three guards were standing by the main door of the Gathering Hall as Doon and Lina went out. The chief guard moved aside to make way for them, and they went through the door and out onto the wide front steps. Lina glanced over her shoulder. Before the door swung closed, she saw the chief guard striding toward the reception desk, where Barton Snode was standing up, leaning forward, his eyes shining with important news.

CHAPTER 13

Deciphering the Message

Doon headed for home, and Lina went in the opposite direction across Harken Square. The little group of Believers had gone, but the protesters with their signs continued to pace back and forth. A few of them were still shaking their fists in the air and yelling, but most of them tramped silently, looking tired and discouraged. Lina felt a bit that way, too. Once Doon said he'd seen a door, she was sure that the door he'd found and the door in the Instructions were the same. She had had such hopes for that door in the Pipeworks. But hoping so hard had made her jump to conclusions. She'd gone a little too fast. She always went fast. Sometimes it was a good thing and sometimes not.

Now Doon thought the Instructions were nothing important after all. She didn't want him to be right. She didn't believe he was, even now. But her thoughts felt like a mess of tangled yarn. She needed someone wise and sensible to help her sort things out. She headed for Glome Street.

Though it was nearly six o'clock, she found Clary still in her workroom, at the far end of Greenhouse 1. It was a small, crowded room. Pots and trowels cluttered a high table at one end. Above the table were shelves full of bottles of seeds, and boxes of string, wire and various kinds of powders. Clary's desk was a rickety table, littered with scraps of paper, all of them covered with notes in her neat, round handwriting. Two rickety chairs went with the rickety table, one on each side. Lina sat down facing Clary. 'I have to tell you some important things,' she said. 'And they're all secret.'

'All right,' said Clary. 'I can keep secrets.' She was wearing a patched shirt that had faded from blue to grey. Her short brown hair was tucked behind her ears, and a bit of leaf clung to it on the right-hand side. She folded her arms in front of her on the desk. She looked square and solid.

'The first thing is,' Lina began, 'that I found the Instructions. But Poppy had chewed them up.'

'The Instructions,' said Clary. 'I'm not familiar with them.'

Lina explained. She went on to explain everything – how she'd shown the Instructions to Doon, what they had figured out, how he'd searched the

Pipeworks and found the door, and what he'd seen when he opened the door.

Clary made an unhappy sound and shook her head. 'This is very bad,' she said. 'And sad, too. I remember when the mayor was first starting out. He has always been foolish, but not always wicked. I'm sorry to know that the worst side of him has won out.' Clary's dark brown eyes seemed to grow deeper and sadder. 'There is so much darkness in Ember, Lina. It's not just outside, it's inside us, too. Everyone has some darkness inside. It's like a hungry creature. It wants and wants and *wants* with a terrible power. And the more you give it, the bigger and hungrier it gets.'

Lina knew. She had felt it in Looper's shop as she hovered over the coloured pencils. For a moment, she felt sorry for the mayor. His hunger had grown so big it could never be satisfied. His huge body couldn't contain it. It made him forget everything else.

Clary let out a long breath, and a few of the scraps of paper on her desk fluttered. She ran her fingers through her hair, felt the bit of leaf and plucked it out. Then she said, 'About these Instructions.'

'Oh, yes,' said Lina. 'They might be important, or they might not be. I don't know any more.'

'I'd like to see them, if you'd let me.'

'Of course you can see them – but you'll have to come home with me.'

'I'll come now, if that's all right,' said Clary.

'There's plenty of time before lights out.'

Lina led Clary up the stairs and into her new bed-room at Mrs Murdo's. 'Nice room,' Clary said, looking around with interest. 'And I see you have a sprout.'

'A what?' said Lina.

'Your bean,' said Clary, pointing at the little pot of dirt on the windowsill.

Lina bent to see what Clary was talking about. Sure enough, the dirt was heaving up a little. She touched the pushed-up part, brushed away the dirt, and discovered a pale green loop. It looked like a neck, as if a creature in the bean were trying to escape but hadn't yet managed to pull its head out. Of course she already knew that plants grew from seeds. But to have put that flat white bean in the dirt, to have almost forgotten about it, and now to see it forcing its way up into the air . . .

'It's doing it!' she said. 'It's coming to life!'

Clary nodded, smiling. 'Still amazes me every time I see it,' she said.

Lina brought out the Instructions, and Clary sat down at the table to study them. She puzzled over the patchwork of scraps for a long time, tracing the lines with her finger, murmuring the parts of words.

'What you've figured out so far seems right to me,' she said. 'I think *ip ork* must be Pipeworks. And *iverb nk* must be riverbank. So this bit must be *down riverbank* – then there's a big space here – *to edge*. Edge of what, I wonder? And does it mean down riverbank as in *walk alongside the river*?'

'Yes, I think so,' Lina said.

'Or does it mean go down the riverbank itself, down the bank towards the water? Maybe *edge* means edge of the water.'

'It couldn't mean that. The bank goes straight down like a wall. You couldn't go down to the edge of the water, you'd fall in.' Lina pictured the dark, swift water and shivered.

'This word,' said Clary, putting a finger on the paper. 'Maybe it isn't *edge*, maybe it's something else. It could be hedge. Or pledge. Those don't make much sense. But it could be ledge or wedge.'

Lina saw that Clary was no better at deciphering the puzzle than she was. She sighed and sat down on the end of her bed. 'It's hopeless,' she said.

Clary straightened up quickly. 'Don't say that. This torn-up piece of paper is the most hopeful thing I've ever seen. Do you know what this word is?' She pointed to the word at the top of the paper, *Egres*.

'Someone's name, isn't it? The title would be Instructions for Egreston, or maybe Egresman, or something like that. The person the instructions were for.'

'I don't think so,' said Clary. 'If you add an s to this word, right where this tear in the paper is, you get

170

Egress. Do you know what that means?'

'No,' said Lina.

'It means the way out. It means the exit. The title of this document is *Instructions for Egress.*'

When Clary left, there was still over an hour before lights out. Lina raced across the city to Greengate Square. She glanced in the window of the Small Items shop, where Doon's father was reaching for something on a shelf, and then she dashed up the stairs and knocked on the door of Doon's apartment. Right away, she heard quick steps and Doon opened the door.

'I have something exciting to tell you,' Lina said breathlessly.

'Come in, then.'

Lina went across the cluttered room to stand by a lamp. She pulled from her pocket a tiny piece of paper on which she had written *Egres.* 'Look at this word,' she said.

'It's from the title of the Instructions. Someone's name,' said Doon.

'No,' said Lina. 'It's meant to be Egress, with two "s"s. I showed the Instructions to Clary, and she told me. It means "the way out".'

'The way out!' cried Doon.

'Yes! The way out. The exit. It's instructions for the way out of Ember!'

'So it *is* real,' Doon said.

'It is. We have to figure out the rest. Or as much of the rest as possible. Can you come now?'

He darted into his room, emerged with his jacket, and they ran.

'All right,' said Lina. They were on the floor of the blue-green room at Mrs Murdo's. 'Let's take the first line.' She moved her finger along it slowly.

1. Exp

   riv   ip   ork .

'We know that *ip ork* is Pipeworks,' she said. '*Exp* could be expand, or explore, or expose . . .'

'There's a big space between *Exp* and the rest,' said Doon. 'There must be more words in there.'

'But who knows what they are? Let's move on.' Lina swept her straggly hair impatiently back from her face. 'Look at number two.'

2.   ston marked with E by
r   dge

Lina put her finger on *ston*. 'What could that be?'

'Maybe piston,' said Doon. 'That's part of a machine, like the generator. Or maybe it's astonish.

Or it could be . . .'

'I bet it's just plain stone,' said Lina. 'There's a lot of stone in the Pipeworks.'

Doon had to admit this was probably right. 'So then,' he said, 'it would be stone marked with E . . . ' He frowned at thc next bit. 'This must be river's edge. Stone marked with E by the river's edge.'

They looked at each other in delight. 'E for Egress!' cried Lina. 'E for Exit!'

They bent over the document again. 'There's not much left of this next line,' said Doon.

3.   adde down   iverb nk

         to   edge appr
  eight
      low.

'Just this part – which must say, *down riverbank to edge . . . something.*'

'Edge of water would make sense. But right after *edge* there's *app*. What would that be?' Doon sat back on his heels and gazed up at the ceiling, as if the answer might be there. Lina muttered, 'Down riverbank to edge, edge.' She thought of Clary's guesses about that line. 'Maybe it's ledge,' she said. 'Down riverbank to ledge. There could be a ledge down near the water.'

'Yes, that must be right. There's a stone marked with E, and down the riverbank at that point there's a ledge. I think we're getting it.'

Once again they crouched over the page, their heads close together. 'OK,' Doon said. 'Line four.'

```
4.                                acks to the
     wat  r,            find door of bo
         ker. Kè                 hind small
     steel  pan     the right              .
     Rem
         ey, open do    .
```

'This is where it says "door",' Lina said. 'Somehow the door is by the ledge. Does that make sense?'

'And there's that small steel pan – what can that mean? What would a pan have to do with anything?'

'But look, but look.' Lina tapped the paper urgently. 'Here it says *ke* and here it says *ey*. It's talking about a key!'

'But what it is a door *to*?' said Doon, sitting back. 'Remember, we thought about this before. A door in the bank of the river would lead *under* the Pipeworks.'

Lina pondered this. 'Maybe it leads to a long tunnel that goes way out beyond Ember, and then gradually up and up until it comes out at the other city.'

'What other city?' Doon glanced up at the drawings tacked to the walls of Lina's room. 'Oh,' he said. 'You mean *that* city.'

'Well, it could be.'

Doon shrugged. 'I suppose so. Or it could be another city exactly like this one.'

That was a gloomy thought. Both of them felt their spirits sink a little at the idea. So they turned back to the task of deciphering.

'Next line,' said Lina.

But Doon sat back on his heels again. He stared into the air, half smiling. 'I have an idea,' he said. 'If we *do* find the way out, we'll need to announce it to everyone. Wouldn't it be splendid to do it during the Singing? Stand up there in front of the whole city and say we've found it?'

'It would be,' Lina said. 'But that's only two days away.'

'Yes. We have to hurry.'

They were bending again over the glued-down fragments when Doon remembered that he should check the time. It was a quarter to nine. He barely had time to get home.

'Come again tomorrow,' said Lina. 'And while you're at work, look for the rock marked with E.'

That night, Doon had trouble sleeping. He couldn't find a comfortable position on his bed. It seemed to be made up of nothing but lumps and wrinkles, and it squeaked and groaned every time he moved. He flailed around so much that the noise woke his father, who came to his room and asked, 'What *is* it, son? Nightmares?'

'No,' said Doon. 'Just can't sleep.'

'Are you worrying? Frightened of anything?'

Doon wanted to say, Yes, Father. I'm worried because the mayor of our city is taking for himself the things that people need, and I'm afraid because any day our lights could go out for ever. I'm worried and afraid a lot of the time, but I'm also excited because I think there *is* a way out, and we might find it – and all those feelings are whirling around in my head, which makes it hard to sleep.

He could have told his father everything. His father would have plunged in with great enthusiasm. He would have helped them decipher the Instructions and expose the mayor's thievery; he would even have come down into the Pipeworks and helped search for the rock marked with E. But Doon wanted to keep these things to himself for now. Tomorrow, the guards would announce that an alert young boy had uncovered the mayor's crime, and his father, hearing the announcements along with the rest of Ember, would turn to the person next to him and say, 'That's my son they're talking about! My *son*!'

So in answer to his father's question, he simply said, 'No, Father, I'm all right.'

'Well, then, see if you can't lie still,' said his father. 'Good night, son,' he added, and closed the door. Doon smoothed out his covers and pulled them up to his chin. He closed his eyes. But still he couldn't sleep.

So he tried a method that had often worked for him before. He would choose a place he knew well – the school, for instance – and imagine himself walking through it, picturing it as he went in minute detail. Often his thoughts would wander, but he would always bring them back to the imaginary journey, and something about doing this would often make him sleepy. This night he decided to retrace his explorations of the Pipeworks. He held his mind to the task for a long time, picturing, with all the clarity he could muster, everything he had seen in that underground realm – the long stairway, the tunnels, the door, the path along the river, the rocks along the path. He felt sleep drawing closer, a heaviness in his limbs, but just as he was about to give in to it, he saw in his mind's eye the wrinkled rocks that bordered the river at the west end of the Pipeworks, the rocks whose strange ridges and creases had reminded him of writing. His eyes flew open in the dark, his heart began to hammer and he gave up on sleeping and lay in a state of terrible impatience for the rest of the night.

CHAPTER 14

The Way Out

The next day was Song Rehearsal Day. Everyone was let off from work at twelve o'clock to practise for the Singing. It was a slow morning for messages. Lina had a lot of time to sit at her station in Garn Square and think. She put her elbows on her knees, rested her chin in her hands and stared down at the pavement in front of the bench, which was worn smooth by the many feet that had passed there. She thought about the mayor, down in his room full of plunder, gorging on peaches and asparagus and wrapping his huge body in elegant new clothes. She thought of his great stack of light bulbs and shook her head in bewilderment. What was he thinking? If he still had light bulbs when everyone else in Ember had run out, would he enjoy sitting in his lit room while the rest of the city drowned in darkness? And when the power finally ran out for good, all his light bulbs would be useless. Possessions couldn't save him – how could he have forgotten that? He must be thinking the same way as

Looper: everything was hopeless anyhow, so he'd live it up while he could.

She leaned back against the bench, stretched her legs out and took a long breath. Very soon, the guards would storm into the secret room and seize the mayor as he sat stuffing himself on stolen goodies. Maybe they already had. Maybe today the stunning news would come: Mayor Arrested! Stealing from Citizens! Maybe they'd announce it at the Singing, so everyone could hear it.

No one came with any messages to be delivered, so after a while Lina left her station and found a step to sit on in an alley off Calloo Street. She pulled back her hair and braided it to keep it from sliding around. Then she took from her pocket the copy of the Instructions she'd made just after she sent her note to the mayor. She unfolded it and began to study it.

This is what she was doing when, a little before twelve o'clock, she looked up to see Doon running towards her. He must have come straight from the Pipeworks – he had a big damp patch of water on one leg of his pants. He spoke in an excited rush. 'I've been looking all over for you!' he said. 'I've found it!'

'Found what?'

'The E! At least it looks like an E. It *must* be an E, though you wouldn't know it if you weren't looking for it . . . '

'You mean the rock marked with an E? In the Pipeworks?'

'Yes, yes, I found it!' He stood breathing hard, his eyes blazing. 'I'd seen it before, but I didn't think of it as an E then, just a squiggle that looked like writing. There are all these rocks that look like they're covered with writing.'

'Which rocks? Where is it?' Lina was on her feet now, bouncing with excitement.

'Down at the west end of the river. Near where it goes into that great hole in the Pipeworks wall.' He paused, trying to catch his breath. 'And listen,' he said. 'We could go there right now.'

'Right now?'

'Yes, because of rehearsals. Everyone's going home, so the Pipeworks will be closed and empty.'

'But if it's closed, how will we get in?'

Grinning, Doon produced a large key from his pocket. 'I ducked into the office on my way out and borrowed the spare key,' he said. 'Lister – he's the Pipeworks director – was in the bathroom practising his singing. He won't miss the key today. And tomorrow, everyone will be off work.' He did an impatient shuffle. 'So come on,' he said.

The town clock struck the first of its twelve noon-time booms. Lina stuffed her copy of the Instructions back in her pocket. 'Let's go.'

* * *

The Pipeworks was empty and silent. Lina and Doon went up the hallway past the rows of boots and the slickers hanging on their hooks. They didn't take any of these for themselves. This was not a Pipeworks tunnel they were about to enter, they were sure; it wouldn't be dripping with water or lined with spurting pipes.

They went down the long stairway and out into the main tunnel, where the river thundered alongside the path, its dark surface strewn with flecks of light.

Doon led the way along the river's edge. As they neared the west end, Lina saw the rocky outcroppings Doon had described to her. They were strange bulging shapes creased with lines like the faces of the very old. Not far beyond, Lina could see the place where the river disappeared into a great hole in the Pipeworks wall.

Doon knelt down beside a clump of stones. He ran a finger over their convoluted surface. 'Look here,' he said. Lina stooped down and peered at the deeply carved lines. It was hard to see the E at first, because it was surrounded by such a tangle of other lines, and because she was expecting it to be an E drawn with straight strokes. But once she saw it – an E drawn with curving lines, a script E – she was sure it had been carved on purpose: it was centred on its stone, and its lines were deep and even.

'So from here we should look down at the river,'

said Doon. 'That's what the Instructions said, down riverbank to ledge.'

He lay on his stomach next to the rock and inched forward until his head hung out over the edge of the path. Lina watched him anxiously. His elbows stuck up on either side of him, and his head, bent down, was nearly invisible. He stayed that way for long seconds. Then he shouted, 'Yes! I see something!' and scrambled to his feet again. 'You do it,' he said. 'Look at the riverbank right below us.'

Lina did as he had. She lay down and pulled herself forward until her head was over the edge. Eight feet or so below her, she saw the black water churning by. She tucked her chin in and looked at the riverbank. It was a sheer rock wall, straight up and down and slick with spray, and at first that was all she saw. But she kept looking and before long could make out short iron bars bolted into the bank, one below the next, almost directly below her. They were like the rungs of a ladder. They *were* a ladder, she realized. The bars provided a way to climb down the riverbank. Not a very appealing way – the bars looked slippery, and the water below was so terribly fast. And because of the dimness and the flying spray, she couldn't actually see if there was a ledge at the bottom or not. But the E was clearly an E, and the bars were clearly a ladder. This must be the right place.

'Who'll go first?' said Doon.

'You can,' Lina said, getting to her feet and stepping away.

'All right.' Doon turned so that his back was to the river, and he eased himself carefully over the rocks, feeling for the first rung with his foot. Lina watched as he sank out of sight, little by little. After a few moments his voice called up from below: 'I'm down! Now you come!'

Lina inched backwards, just as Doon had, letting one foot dangle over the edge, lower and lower, until it touched the first rung of the ladder. She shifted her weight to that foot, clinging with cold fingers to a ridge in the rock, and lowered herself slowly until she was standing on the rung with both feet. Her heart was beating so hard she was afraid it would shake her fingers loose from their grip.

Now she had to move downwards. She felt for the next rung with her foot, found it, let herself down. It would have been easy if it hadn't been for the river waiting below to swallow her.

'You're almost here!' called Doon. His voice came from right below her. 'There's a ledge – one more rung and you'll feel it.'

She did feel it, solid beneath her foot. For a second, she stood there, still clutching the ladder. The surging water was only inches below her now. Don't think about it, she told herself. She moved sideways two steps to stand next to Doon, and there in front of them was a rectangular space carved out of the river wall, rather like the entry hall of a building. It was perhaps eight feet wide and eight feet high, and would have been invisible from anywhere else in the Pipeworks. You had to have climbed down the riverbank to see it.

They stepped into this entry hall and walked a few steps. Enough light to see by came from the tunnel behind them.

Lina stopped. 'There's the door!' she said.

'What?' said Doon. The water roared so loudly they had to shout to be heard.

'The door!' Lina yelled happily.

'Yes!' Doon yelled back. 'I see it!'

At the end of the passage was a wide, solid-looking door. It was dull grey, mottled with greenish and brownish blotches that looked like mildew. Lina put her palms against it. It was metal, and it felt cold. The door had a metal handle, and just below the handle was a keyhole.

Lina reached into the pocket of her trousers for her copy of the Instructions. She unfolded it, and Doon looked over her shoulder. Together they squinted at the paper in the dim light from the main tunnel.

'This is the part, right here,' she said, pointing:

3.   adde down iverb nk

      to   edge appr
eight
      low.
4.   acks to the
    wat r,   find door of bo
        ker. Ke   hind small
  steel pan   the right   .
Rem
      ey, open do .

Lina ran her finger along line number 3. 'This must say, *Something something down riverbank to ledge approximately eight feet below*. That's what we've just done. Then four is something about . . . *backs to the water, find door . . . something*. And then *Ke hind* – that must be key behind, and then there's the small steel pan. Do you see a small steel pan?'

Doon was still studying the paper. 'It says right. We should look to the right of the door.'

And quite easily they found it. It wasn't a pan at all, but a small square of steel embedded in the wall. 'A steel *panel*,' said Lina. She ran her fingers across it and felt a dent at one side. When she pressed there, the panel sprang open easily and silently, as if it were glad to have been finally found. Inside, a silver key was hanging on a hook.

Lina reached for it and then drew her hand back. 'Shall I do it?' she said. 'Or shall you?'

'You do it,' said Doon.

So she took the key from its hook and put it in the keyhole. She turned it and felt a click. She grasped the door handle and pushed, but nothing happened. She pushed harder. 'It won't budge,' she said.

'Maybe it opens outward,' said Doon.

Lina pulled. The door still didn't move. 'It *has* to open,' she said. 'We unlocked it!' She pulled and pushed and hauled on the handle – and the door moved, not inward or outward but sideways. 'Oh, *this* is how it goes!' cried Lina. She pulled the handle to the left, and with a deep rasping sound, the door slid away, into a slot in the wall. Behind it was a space of utter darkness.

They stared. Lina had expected to see something when the door opened. She had thought there would be light behind it, and a path or road.

'Shall we go in?' said Lina.

Doon nodded.

Lina stepped across the threshold. The air had a dank, stuffy smell. She turned to the right and put her right hand against the wall. It was smooth and flat. The floor, too, was smooth.

'There might be a light switch,' she said. She patted the wall just inside the door, from the floor to as high as she could reach, but found nothing.

Doon turned left and felt on the other side, with the same result. 'Nothing,' he said.

Very slowly, keeping a hand to the wall and tapping the floor cautiously with their feet before every step, Doon and Lina made their way in opposite directions. Each of them soon came to a corner and turned again. Now they were going deeper into the dark. They both had the same thought: Is the way out of Ember a long dark tunnel? Must we go mile after mile in absolute darkness?

But suddenly Lina gave a yelp of surprise. 'Something's here on the floor,' she said. Her foot had banged against a hard object. She knelt down and touched it cautiously with her hands. It was a metal cube, about a foot square. 'It's a box, I think. Two boxes,' she added as she explored farther.

Doon took a step towards her in the darkness, and his knees banged into a hard edge. 'There's something else here, too,' he said. 'Not a box.' He ran his hands along it. 'It's big and has a curved edge.'

'The boxes are small enough to lift,' said Lina. 'Let's take them out where it's lighter and see what they are. Come and help.'

Doon made his way to Lina and picked up one of the boxes. They walked back through the door and set the boxes down a few feet from the river's edge. They were made of dark green metal and had grey metal handles on top and a kind of latch on the side. The latches opened easily. Lina and Doon raised the hinged lids and looked inside.

What they saw puzzled and disappointed them. Lina's box was full of smooth white rods, each about ten inches long. At the end of each one, a little bit of string poked out. In Doon's box were dozens of small packets wrapped in a slippery material. He opened one and found a lot of short wooden sticks, each with a blue blob on the end. Both boxes had a label on the inside of the lid. The label on Lina's box said 'Candles'. The label on Doon's said 'Matches', and under it was a white, inch-wide strip of some kind of rough, pebbly material.

'What does "Candles" mean?' Lina said, puzzled. She took out one of the white rods. It felt slick, almost greasy.

'And what does "Matches" mean?' said Doon. 'Matches what?' He took one of the small sticks from its packet. The blue stuff on the end was not wood. 'Could it be something to write with? Like a pencil? Maybe it writes blue.'

'But what's the point of a whole box of tiny pencils?' asked Lina. 'I don't understand.'

Doon frowned at the little blue-tipped stick. 'I don't see what else it could be,' he said finally. 'I'll try writing something with it.'

'On what?'

Doon looked around. The floor was too damp from the spray of the river to write on. 'I could try it on the Instructions,' he said. Lina handed them to him. Carefully, he rubbed the blue end of the stick along the edge of the paper. It didn't leave a mark. He rubbed it along his arm. No mark there, either.

'Try this white stuff,' Lina said, pointing to the white strip inside the lid of the box.

He scraped the blue tip across the rough surface. Instantly, the end of the stick burst into flame. Doon cried out and flung the stick away. It landed on the floor a few feet off, where it burned brightly for a moment and then sputtered out.

They stared at each other, their mouths open in astonishment. There was a strange sharp smell in the air that smarted in their noses.

'It makes fire!' said Doon. 'And light!'

'Let me try one,' said Lina. She took a stick from the box and ran it across the rough strip. It blazed up fiercely, but she managed to hold onto it for a moment. Then she felt the heat on her fingers and let go, and the flaming stick dropped over the ledge and into the river.

'Firesticks,' said Doon. 'Are they what saves Ember?'

'I don't see how they could be,' said Lina. 'They're so small. They go out too fast.' She shivered. This was not turning out the way she'd thought it would. She held up one of the white things. 'Anyway, what are these for?'

Doon shook his head in bewilderment. 'Maybe a

candle is a kind of handle,' he said. 'Maybe you tie the stick on with the string, and then you can hold it longer while it burns.'

'It would still go out just as fast,' Lina said.

'Yes,' said Doon. 'But it's all I can think of. Let's try it.'

With a great deal of effort, they looped the string of a rod around one of the sticks. Lina held the rod while Doon scraped the blue tip into flame. They watched the stick flare brightly, making shadows jump up behind them. The wood turned black, and the charred firestick crumbled and dropped to the ground. But the light didn't go out. The string itself had caught fire. As they watched, it sputtered and smoked and then burned steadily, filling the little room with a warm glow.

'It's the moveable light,' said Doon in awe.

All Lina's excitement flooded back. 'And now, and now,' she said, 'we can go back into the room and see what's there.'

They went back down the passage to the doorway and stepped inside. Lina held the moveable light at arm's length before her. In its flickering glow they saw something made of silvery metal. They walked slowly around, examining it. It was long and low, filling up the centre of the room. One end of it came to a point. The other end was flat. Across the open middle stretched two metal strips. Four stout ropes were attached to the outside, one at each end and one on each side. And on the floor of the thing were two poles, each flattened at one end.

'Look,' said Lina. 'There's a word on its side.' They squatted at the pointed end and held the flame near the word. It said, in square black letters, 'BOAT'.

'Boat,' repeated Doon. 'What does that mean?'

'I don't know,' said Lina. 'And here's another word, on these poles: Paddles. The only paddle I know is the one Mrs Polster uses on kids who misbehave in school.'

Once again, she took her copy of the Instructions from her pocket and consulted it, holding it in the light of the flame. 'Look,' she said, 'right here: *oat* must be boat.'

```
5.              oat,    stocked
with nec        uip ent.
Bac
     ont  s     eet.
```

'And the next part must say, stocked with necessary equipment,' said Doon. 'That must be what's in the boxes.'

'Then there's this.' Lina ran her finger along the next line.

6. Usi   opes, lowe

ter. Head dow st   . Us pa

av   cks and assist over rap   .

'This word must be ropes,' she said. 'Then lower
. . . and then . . . would this word be downstairs?
Maybe it says, head downstairs?'

'That doesn't make sense,' said Doon. 'There
aren't any stairs, except the ones that go up.' He
frowned at the word, and then he took a short, sharp
breath. 'Downstream,' he said. 'The word must be
downstream. It must say something like, *Use the ropes
to lower the boat, and head downstream.*' He looked up
at Lina and spoke in a voice full of wonder. 'The boat
goes on the water. It's something to ride in.'

They stared at each other in the flickering light,
realizing what this meant. There was no tunnel leading out of Ember. The way out was the river. To leave
Ember, they must go on the river.

CHAPTER 15

A Desperate Run

'But this can't be right,' said Doon. 'If the river is the way out of Ember, why is there just one boat? It's only big enough for two people.'

'I don't know,' said Lina. 'It *is* strange.'

'Let's look around some more.'

They stood up. Doon went back to where they'd left the boxes and got another candle. He brought it into the boat room and lit it, and the room grew twice as bright. Right away they saw what they hadn't noticed before: in the back wall was a door almost as wide as the whole room. When they went up to it they could see that it, too, was a sliding door. Doon took hold of the handle that was on the right and pulled sideways, and the door rolled smoothly open to reveal more darkness.

They stepped in. They could guess from the echoing sound of their voices when they spoke that they were in a tremendous room, though the ceiling was low – they could see it just over their heads. The candlelight glinted off something shiny, and as they went in farther they could see that the room was filled with boats, row upon row of them, all just like the one in the first room. 'There must be hundreds,' Lina whispered.

'Enough for everyone, I suppose,' said Doon.

They wandered around a bit, but there wasn't really much to see. All the boats were the same. Each one contained two metal boxes and two paddles. The room was cold, and the air felt heavy in their lungs. The candle flames burned weakly. So they went back to the small room and slid the door closed behind them. 'I guess,' said Lina, 'that this first boat is meant as a sort of sample. We learn what's what on the one that has signs. Boat. Paddles. Candles. Matches.'

They went back out to the river's edge. Lina blew out her candle and began closing up the boxes they'd opened.

Doon blew out his, too. 'I'm going to take my candle with me,' he said, 'to look at later. I want some matches as well.' He took a packet of matches from the box and tucked it inside his shirt.

Lina returned the boxes to the boat room and slid the door closed. Then she and Doon stood together on the ledge and gazed down. Less than a foot below, the river rushed by. A short distance downstream it plunged into the dark mouth in the wall and disappeared.

'Well,' he said, 'we've found it.'

'We've found it,' Lina repeated, wonderingly.

'And tomorrow, at the start of the Singing,' said Doon, 'we'll stand up in Harken Square and tell the whole city.'

When they came up out of the Pipeworks, it was nearly six o'clock. They hadn't realized they'd been down there so long; both Doon's father and Mrs Murdo would be wondering where they were. They stood for a moment under a lamppost, just long enough to agree on a time to meet the next day and plan their announcement. Then they hurried home. When Doon's father asked why he was so late, he said his song rehearsal had gone on for a long time. He wanted to shout out to his father, *We've found the way out! We're saved!* But he held himself in for the sake of his moment of glory. Tomorrow, when his father saw him on the steps of the Gathering Hall, he would be so overcome with surprise and pride that he would go weak in the knees, and the people standing next to him would have to catch him and hold him up.

And the announcement about the thieving mayor! That would probably happen tomorrow, too. Doon had almost forgotten it in the excitement of finding the boats. The mayor's arrest and the city's rescue, both at once! It was going to be an amazing day. Racing thoughts kept Doon awake almost until morning.

The day of the Singing was a holiday for the entire city; all the stores and other businesses were closed. This meant that Doon didn't have to go to the Pipeworks. His father didn't have to go to his shop, either, but he was going to go anyhow. If he wasn't in his shop, fussing with his merchandise, he didn't know what to do with himself.

Doon dawdled over his breakfast of carrot sticks and mashed turnips, waiting for his father to go. He wanted to get ready for the journey down the river. They probably wouldn't leave for a few days – he and Lina would make their announcement tonight, and people would need time to get organized before they could leave the city – but he was too excited to sit around doing nothing.

As soon as his father left, Doon slipped the case off his pillow. This would be his travelling pack. He put in the candle and the matches. He put in the key he'd borrowed from the Pipeworks office. He put in a good-sized piece of rope that he'd found at the trash heaps and had been saving for years and a bottle for water. He put in an ancient folding knife that his father had given him, which had come down through generations of his family and which he used to chop off his fringe when it got so long it tickled his eyelids. He put in some extra clothes, in case he got wet, and some paper and a pencil, so that he could write a record of the journey. Along with these things, he crammed in a small blanket – it might be cold in the new city – and a packet of food: six carrots, a handful of vitamins, some peas and mushrooms wrapped in a lettuce leaf, two boiled beets and two boiled turnips. That should be enough. Surely, when they got to where they were going, the people who lived there would give them something to eat. He tied the top of the pillowcase in a knot, and then he untied it again. He might want to add something else.

He stood in the middle of the apartment and looked around at the jumble of stuff. There was nothing else here that he wanted to take with him – no, there was one thing. He went back into his room. From beneath his bed he pulled out the pages of his bug book. He leafed through it. The white spider. The moth with the zigzag pattern on its wings. The bee, striped brown and yellow on its rear end. He looked at his drawings for a long time, memorizing their beauty and strangeness. Tiny fringes of hair, minute claws, jointed legs. Should he take this with him? There might not be creatures like this where they were going. He might never see such things again.

But no, he'd leave it behind – his pack should be small and light. He put the bug book back under his bed and pulled out the box where he kept the green worm. He drew back the scarf to check his captive one more time. Several days before, the worm had done a curious thing: it had wrapped itself up in a blanket of threads. Since then it had hung motionless from a bit of cabbage stem. Doon had been watching it carefully. Either it was dead, or it was undergoing the change that he'd read about in a library book but could hardly believe was true – the change from a crawling thing to a flying thing. So far, the bundled-up worm had shown no signs of life.

But now he saw that it was wriggling. The whole wrapped-up bundle, which was shaped like a large vitamin pill, bent slightly from side to side, then was still, then bent back and forth again. Something was pushing at the top end of it, and in a moment the threads there split apart and a dark furry knob emerged. Doon watched, holding his breath. Next came two hairlike legs, which clawed and plucked at the blanket. In a few minutes the whole creature was out. Egress, thought Doon with a smile. The creature's wings were crushed flat against its body at first, but soon they opened, and Doon saw what his green worm had become: a moth with light brown wings. He lifted the box and carried it to the window. He opened the window and held the box out into the air. The moth waved its feathery feelers and took a few steps along the wilted cabbage leaf. For several minutes, it stood still, its wings trembling slightly. Then it fluttered up into the air, rising higher and higher until it was just a pale spot against the dark sky.

Doon watched until the moth disappeared. He

knew he had seen something marvellous. What was the power that turned the worm into a moth? It was greater than any power the Builders had had, he was sure of that. The power that ran the city of Ember was feeble by comparison – and about to run out.

For a few minutes he stood by the window, looking out over the square and thinking again about what to pack for his journey. Should he put in anything like nails or wire? Would he need money? Should he take some soap?

Then he laughed and struck a hand against his head. He kept forgetting that the entire population of the city would be with him on the trip. If he needed something he didn't have, someone would surely be able to supply it.

So he tied a knot in his pillowcase and was about to close the window when he caught sight of three burly men wearing the red and brown uniform of the city guards striding into the square. They stopped and looked around for a moment. Then one of them confronted old humpbacked Nammy Proggs, who was standing not far from the entrance to the Small Items shop. The guard towered over her, and she twisted her head sideways and squinted up at him. Doon could hear the guard's voice clearly: 'We're looking for a boy named Harrow.'

'Why?' said Nammy.

'Spreading vicious rumours,' was the answer.

'Do you know where he is?'

Nammy hesitated a moment, and then she said, 'Went off to the trash heaps just a minute ago.' The guard nodded curtly and beckoned to his companions. They marched away.

Spreading vicious rumours! Doon was so stunned that he stood still as stone for a long minute. What could they possibly mean? But there was only one answer. It had to be what they'd told the assistant guard about the mayor. Why were they calling it a vicious rumour? It was the truth! He didn't understand it.

He did understand, though, that Nammy Proggs had done him a favour. She must have seen that the guards meant him no good. She had protected him, at least for the moment, by sending the guards to the wrong place.

Doon forced his mind to slow down and think. Why did the guards think he and Lina were lying? Obviously, they hadn't investigated the room in Tunnel 351. If they had, they'd have known he and Lina were telling the truth.

He could think of only one other possibility. The guards – at least some of them – already knew what the mayor was doing. They knew about it and wanted it to stay a secret. And why? It was clear: the guards, too, were getting things from the storerooms.

It had to be the answer. For a moment, the fear he'd felt when he saw the guards was replaced by rage. The familiar hot wave rose in him, and he wanted to grab a handful of his father's nails or pot shards and throw them against the wall. But all at once he remembered: if the guards were after him, they'd be after Lina, too. He had to warn her. He dashed down the stairs, his anger turning into power for his running feet.

After they discovered the room full of boats, Lina had come home to Mrs Murdo's with the sound of the river still in her ears. It was like a huge, powerful voice, roaring at the top of its lungs. Deep inside herself Lina felt an answering call, as if she, too, contained a drop of the same power. She would ride on the river – she could hardly believe it – and it might take her to the shining city she had dreamed of, or it might drown her. What she had imagined before – the smooth, gently sloping path leading out – now seemed childish. How could the way into a new world be so easy? She dreaded going on the river, but she was ready for it, too. She longed to go.

She slept that night in the beautiful blue-green room, in the big lumpy bed with Poppy next to her. She felt safe here. Mrs Murdo came in and tucked the covers around her. She sat on the edge of the bed and sang an odd little song to Poppy – something about rock-a-bye baby, in the treetops. 'What are treetops?' Lina asked, but Mrs Murdo didn't know. 'It's a very old song,' she said. 'It's probably nonsense words.'

She said good night and went out into the living room, where Lina could hear her humming quietly as she tidied up. She was so orderly. She never left her stockings draped over the back of a chair, or her sewing spread out all over the table. Lina closed her eyes and waited for sleep.

But her thoughts kept tumbling around. So much was going to happen tomorrow – the whole city would be in an uproar. People would stream down into the Pipeworks to see the boats. They'd be excited, shouting and laughing and crying, packing up their belongings, and surging through the streets. If they couldn't all fit into the boats, there would be fights. Some people might get hurt. It was going to be a mess. She'd have to keep her little family close around her – Poppy, Mrs Murdo and Doon, and perhaps Doon's father and Clary. Through it all, she would hold tight to Poppy so no harm could come to her.

It seemed she had barely closed her eyes when she felt Poppy's hard little heels banging against her shins. 'Time-a get up! Get up!' Poppy chirped.

She got out of bed and dressed herself and Poppy. In the kitchen, Mrs Murdo was mashing potatoes for breakfast. How lovely, Lina thought, to have breakfast cooked for her – to hear water bubbling in the pot, and to find a bowl and a spoon set out on the table, and vitamins lined up neatly beside a cup of beet tea. I could live here for ever, Lina thought, before she remembered that in a day or two they would all be leaving.

There was a sudden banging on the front door. Mrs Murdo dried her hands and went to answer it, but before she'd taken three steps the banging came again. 'I'm coming, I'm coming,' Mrs Murdo cried, and when she opened the door, there was Doon.

His face was flushed, and he was breathing hard. He had a bulging pillowcase slung over his shoulder.

He looked past Mrs Murdo to Lina. 'I have to talk to you,' he said. 'Right now, but . . .' He threw a doubtful glance at Mrs Murdo.

Lina scrambled up from the table. 'In here,' she said, towing him towards the blue-green room.

When she had closed the door, Doon told her what had happened. 'They'll come for you, too,' he said, 'any minute. We have to get out of here. We have to hide from them.'

Lina could hardly make sense of what he was saying. They were in *trouble*? Her legs went shaky at the knees. 'Hide?' she said. 'Hide where?'

'We could go to the school – no one would be there today – or the library. It's almost always open, even on holidays.' He hopped impatiently from foot to foot. 'But we have to go *fast*, we have to go *now*. They have *signs* up about us all over the city!'

'Signs?'

'Telling people to report us if they see us!'

Lina felt as if a swarm of insects was inside her head, buzzing so loudly she couldn't think. 'How long do we have to hide? All day?'

'I don't know – we don't have time to think about it. Lina, they could be outside the door *this minute.*'

The urgency in his voice convinced her. On the way through the living room she gave Poppy a quick kiss and called, 'Bye, Mrs Murdo. We have some emergency work to do. If anyone comes asking for me, say I'll be back later.' They were down the stairs before Mrs Murdo could ask any questions.

Once in the street, they ran. 'Where to?' Lina said.

'The school,' Doon answered.

They took Greystone Street, staying within the shadows as much as they could. As they passed the shoe shop, Lina saw a white piece of paper stuck up on the window. She glanced at it and her heart gave a wild jump. Her name and Doon's were written on it in big black letters:

DOON HARROW AND LINA MAYFLEET
WANTED FOR SPREADING VICIOUS RUMOURS
IF YOU SEE THEM,
REPORT TO MAYOR'S CHIEF GUARD.
BELIEVE NOTHING THEY SAY.
REWARD

She snatched the poster off the window, crumpled it up and tossed it into the nearest trash can. In the next block, she tore down two more, and Doon ripped one off a lamppost. But there were too many to get them all, and they didn't have time to waste.

They ran faster. On this holiday, people slept late, and because the stores were closed, the streets were nearly empty. Still, they took the long route all the way out by the beehives to avoid Sparkswallow Square, where a few people might be standing around and talking. They ran past the greenhouses and up Dedlock Street. As they crossed Night Street, Lina glanced to her left. Two blocks away, a couple of guards were crossing to Greengate Square. She tapped Doon's shoulder and pointed. He saw, and they ran faster. Had they been noticed? Lina thought not; they would have heard a shout if the guards had seen them.

They got to the school and went in through the back door. In the Wide Hallway, their footsteps echoed on the wooden floor. It was strange to be here again, and to be here alone, without the clatter and chatter of other children. The hallway with its eight doors seemed smaller to Lina than it had when she was a student, and shabbier. The planks of the floor were scuffed grey, and there was a cloud of finger smudges around the doorknob of every door.

They went into Miss Thorn's room and, out of habit, sat at their old desks. 'I don't think they'll look for us here,' said Doon. 'If they do, we can crawl into the paper cabinet.' He set his pack down next to him on the floor.

For a while they just sat there, getting their breath back. They hadn't turned the light on, so the room was dim – the only light came from beneath the blind over the window.

'Those posters,' Lina said after a while.

'Yes. Everyone will see them.'

'What will they do to us if they catch us?'

'I don't know. Something to keep us from telling what we know. Put us in the Prison Room, maybe.'

Lina ran her finger along the B carved in the desktop. It felt like a very long time since she'd last sat at this desk. 'We can't hide in here for ever,' she said.

'No,' said Doon. 'Just until it's time for the Singing. Then when everyone is gathered in Harken Square, we'll go and tell about the boats and the mayor. Won't we? I haven't really thought about it – I haven't had a chance to think at all this morning.'

'But the guards are always there at the Singing, standing next to the mayor,' said Lina. 'They'd grab us as soon as we opened our mouths.'

Doon's eyebrows came together in a dark line. 'You're right. So what will we do?'

It was like finding yourself on a dead-end street, Lina thought. There was no way out. She stared blankly at the things that had once been her daily companions – the teacher's desk, the stacks of paper, *The Book of the City of Ember* on its special shelf. The old words ran through her head: 'There is no place but Ember. Ember is the only light in the dark world.' She knew now that this wasn't true. There *was* someplace else – the place where the boats would take them.

As if Doon had read her thoughts, he looked up. 'We could go.'

'Go where?' she said, though she knew right away what he meant.

'Wherever the river leads,' he said. He gestured to the pillowcase sack. 'I packed up my bag this morning – I'm all ready. I'm sure I have enough for you, too.'

Lina felt her heart shrink a little. 'Go by ourselves?' she said. 'Without telling anyone?'

'We *will* tell them.' Doon was on his feet now. He went to the cabinet and got a sheet of paper. 'We'll write a note explaining everything – a note to someone we trust, someone who'll believe us.'

'But I can't just leave,' said Lina. 'How could I leave Poppy? And not even say goodbye to her? Not know where I'm going, or if I'm ever coming back? How could *you* go without saying goodbye to your father?'

'Because,' said Doon, 'once they find the boats, the rest of Ember will follow us. It's not as if we're leaving them for ever.' He strode across the room and rummaged in Miss Thorn's desk. 'Who shall we write the message to?'

Lina wasn't sure about this idea, but she couldn't, at the moment, think of a better one. So she said, 'We could write it to Clary. She's seen the Instructions. She'll believe what we say. And she lives close by – just up in Torrick Square.'

'OK,' said Doon. He pulled a pencil from the desk drawer. 'Really,' he said, 'this is a perfect idea. We can get away from the guards and leave our message behind us. *And* we can be the first ones to arrive in the new city! We *should* be the first, because we discovered the way.'

'Well, that's true.' Lina thought for a minute. 'How long do you think it will take before the rest of them find the boats and come? It's a lot of people to get organized.' She numbered on her fingers the things that would have to happen. 'Clary will have to get the head of the Pipeworks to go down with her and find the boats. Then she'll have to make the announcement to the city. Then everyone in Ember will have to pack up their things, troop down to the river, get all those boats out of that big room and load themselves in. It could be a big mess, Doon. Poppy will need me.' She pictured frenzied crowds of people, and Poppy tiny and lost among them.

'Poppy has Mrs Murdo,' said Doon. 'She'll be fine. Really. Mrs Murdo is very organized.'

It was true. The thought of taking Poppy with her on the river, which had darted into Lina's mind, darted out again. I'm only being selfish, she thought, to want to have her with me. It's too dangerous to take her. Mrs Murdo will bring her in a day or two. This seemed the most sensible plan, though it made her so sad that it cast a shadow over the thrill of going to the new city. 'What if something goes wrong?' she said.

'Nothing will go wrong! It's a good plan, Lina. We'll be there ahead of everyone else – we can welcome them when they come, we can show them around!' Doon was bursting with eagerness. His eyes shone, and he jiggled up and down.

'Well, all right,' Lina said. 'Let's write our message, then.'

Doon wrote for a long time. When he was finished, he showed what he'd written to Lina. He'd explained how to find the rock with the E, how to go down to the boat room, even how to use the candles.

'It's good,' she said. 'Now we have to deliver it.' She paused a moment to see if she had any courage inside her. She found that she did, along with sadness and fear and excitement. 'I'll deliver it,' she said. 'I'm the messenger, after all. I know back ways to go, where no one will see me.' An idea struck her. 'Doon, maybe Clary will be home! Maybe she would keep us safe and help us tell what we know, and we won't *have* to leave right now.'

Doon quickly shook his head. 'I doubt it,' he said. 'She's probably with her singing group, getting ready. You'll just have to leave the note under her door.'

Lina could tell from his tone of voice that Doon didn't really want Clary to be home. She supposed he had his heart set on their going down the river by themselves. Doon glanced up at the clock on the schoolroom wall. 'It's a little after two,' he said. 'The Singing begins at three. After that, everyone will be in Harken Square and the streets will be empty. I think we can get to the Pipeworks safely then – why don't we leave about a quarter past three.'

'You still have the key?'

Doon nodded.

'So after I've delivered the note to Clary, I'll come back here,' said Lina.

'Yes. And then we'll wait until three-fifteen, and then we'll go.'

Lina got up from the cramped desk and went to

the window. She moved the blind a little and peered out. There was no one in the street. The dusty schoolroom was very quiet. She thought about Doon's father, who would be frantic when he saw his son's name on those posters and then realized later that Doon had disappeared. She thought about Mrs Murdo, who might already have seen the posters, and who would be frightened if guards came looking for Lina and terrified if Lina didn't come home by nightfall. She tried not to think about Poppy at all; she couldn't bear it.

'Give me the note,' she said to Doon at last. She folded the piece of paper carefully and put it in the pocket of her trousers. 'Back soon,' she said, and went out of the room and down the hall to the rear door of the school.

Doon went to the window to watch her go. He moved the blind aside just enough to see out into Pibb Street. There she was, running in that longlegged way, with her hair flying. She started across Stonegrit Lane. Just before she reached the other side, Doon's breath stopped in his throat. Two guards rounded the corner from Knack Street, directly ahead of her. One of them was the chief guard. He leaped forward and shouted so loudly Doon could hear him plainly through the glass: 'That's her! Get her!'

Lina reversed her direction in an instant. She raced back down Pibb Street, turned down School

Street toward Bilbollio Square and vanished from Doon's sight. The guards ran after her, shouting. Doon watched, sick with horror. She's much faster than they are, he told himself. She'll lose them – she knows places to hide. He stood frozen next to the window, hardly breathing. They won't catch her, he thought. I'm sure they won't catch her.

CHAPTER 16

The Singing

When Lina heard the guards shout, terror shot through her. She ran faster than she ever had before, her heart pounding wildly. Behind her, the guards kept up their shouting, and she knew that if other guards were nearby they would come running. She had to find a hiding place. Ahead of her was Bilbollio Square – was there a spot she could duck into? And like an answer, Doon's words came back to her: 'The library. It's almost always open, even on holidays.' She didn't have time to think. She didn't ask herself whether Edward Pocket would be willing to hide her, or whether there would even *be* a good place to hide in the library. She just ran for the passageway that led to the library door and darted down it.

But the library door wouldn't open. She turned the knob frantically, she pulled and pushed, and then, at the same time that she heard the running footsteps of the guards coming into the square, she saw the small handwritten sign stuck to the door: 'Closed for the Singing'. The guards were very near now. If she ran, they would see her. She flattened herself against the wall, hoping they wouldn't think to look in the library passage.

But they did. 'Here she is!' yelled one of the guards. She tried to shoot past him, but the passage was too narrow, and he caught her by the arm. She pulled and twisted and kicked, but the chief guard had her now, too. He gripped her other arm with fingers that felt like iron. 'Stop your struggling!' he shouted.

Lina reached up and grabbed a handful of his wiry beard. She pulled with all her might, and the chief guard roared, but he didn't let go. He yanked her forward, almost off the ground, and the two guards dragged her across the square at an awkward, lop-sided pace that made her stumble over her own feet.

'You're hurting me!' Lina said. 'Don't hold so tight!'

'Don't you tell us what to do,' said the chief guard. 'We'll hold you tight till we get you where you're going.'

'Where is that?' said Lina. She was so enraged at her bad luck that she almost forgot to be afraid.

'You're going to see the mayor, missy,' said the chief guard. 'He'll decide what to do with you.'

'But I haven't done anything wrong!'

'Spreading vicious rumours,' said the guard.

'Telling dangerous lies calculated to cause civic unrest.'

'It's not a lie!' she said. But the guard gripped her arm even more tightly and gave her a shove so she stumbled sideways.

'No talking,' he said, and they walked the rest of the way in grim silence.

A few people had already gathered in Harken Square, though the workers were still getting it ready for the Singing. Street-sweepers crossed the square back and forth, pushing their brooms. Someone appeared at a second-floor window of a building on Gilly Street and unfurled one of the banners that was always displayed for the Singing – a long piece of red cloth, faded after years of use but still showing its design of wavy lines, representing the river, the source of all power. That was for 'The Song of the River'. There would be a banner on the Broad Street side of the square, too, this one deep yellow-gold with a design like a grid to represent 'The Song of the City'. and another banner on the Otterwill side for 'The Song of Darkness'. perfectly black except for a narrow yellow edge.

The guards marched Lina up the steps of the Gathering Hall and through the wide doorway. They took her down the main corridor, opened the door at the end, and gave her one last push, a push that caused her to stagger forward in an undignified way and bump up against the back of a chair.

It was the same room she'd been in that other, much happier day – her first day as a messenger. Nothing had changed – the frayed red curtains, the armchairs with the upholstery worn thin, the hideous mud-coloured carpet. The portraits on the wall looked down at her sorrowfully.

'Sit there,' said the chief guard. He pointed at a small, hard-looking chair that faced the large armchair. Lina sat. Next to the chair was the small table she remembered from before, with the china teapot and a tray of china teacups with chips around their edges.

The chief guard left the room – to find the mayor, Lina supposed. The other one stood silently with his arms folded across his chest. Nothing happened for a while. Lina tried to think about what she would say to the mayor, but her mind wouldn't work.

Then the door to the front hall opened, and the mayor came in. It was the first time Lina had seen him up close since she had delivered Looper's message to him. He seemed even more immense. His baggy face was the colour of a mushroom. He wore a black suit that stretched only far enough across his vast belly for one button to connect with its buttonhole.

He moved ponderously across the room and settled into the armchair, filling it completely. Next to his chair was a table, and on the table was a brass bell the size of a fist. The mayor gazed for a moment at Lina with eyes that looked like the openings of tunnels, and then he turned to the guard.

'Dismissed,' he said, waving the back of his hand at him. 'Return when I ring the bell.'

The guard left. The mayor swung his gaze back to Lina. 'I am not surprised,' he said. He lifted one arm and pointed a finger at Lina's face. 'You have been in trouble before. Going where you shouldn't.'

Lina started to speak, but the mayor held up his hand. It was an oddly small hand, with short fingers like ripe pea pods.

'Curiosity,' said the mayor. 'A dangerous quality. Unhealthy. Especially regrettable in one so young.'

'I'm twelve,' said Lina.

'Silence!' said the mayor. 'I am speaking.' He wriggled slightly from side to side, wedging himself more firmly into the chair. He'll need to be pried out of it, Lina thought.

'Ember, as you know,' the mayor went on, 'is in a time of difficulty. Extraordinary measures are necessary. This is a time when citizens should be most loyal. Most law-abiding. For the good of all.'

Lina said nothing. She watched how the flesh under the mayor's chin bulged in and out as he spoke, and then she turned her eyes from this unpleasant sight and looked carefully around the room. She was thinking now, calculating, but not about what the mayor was saying.

'The duties of a mayor,' said the mayor, 'are . . . complex. Cannot be understood by regular citizens, particularly children. That is why . . . ' he went on, leaning slightly forward so that his stomach pushed farther out along his lap, 'certain things must remain hidden from the public. The public would not understand. The public must have faith,' said the mayor, once again holding up his hand, this time with a finger pointing to the ceiling, 'that all is being done for their benefit. For their own good.'

'Hogwash,' said Lina.

The mayor jerked backwards. His eyebrows came down over his eyes, making them into dark slits. '*What?*' he said. 'Surely I heard you incorrectly.'

'I said hogwash,' said Lina. 'It means—'

'Do not presume to tell me what it means!' the mayor cried. 'Impudence will make things worse for you.' He was breathing heavily, and his words came out with spaces between them. 'A misguided child . . . such as yourself . . . requires . . . a forceful lesson.' His short fingers gripped the arms of the chair. 'Perhaps,' he said, 'your curiosity has led you to wonder . . . about the Prison Room. What could it be like, eh? Dark? Cold? Uncomfortable?' He made the smile that Lina remembered from Assignment Day. His lips pulled away from his small teeth; his grey cheeks folded. 'You will have a chance to find out.

You will become . . . closely acquainted . . . with the Prison Room. The guards will escort you there. Your accomplice – another known troublemaker – will join you, as soon as he is located.'

The mayor turned to look for the bell. This was the moment when Lina had planned to make a dash for freedom – she thought she had a slim chance to succeed if she moved fast enough – but something happened in that instant that gave her a head start.

The lights went out.

There was no flicker this time, just sudden, complete darkness. It was fortunate that Lina had already planned her move and knew exactly which way to go. She leaped up, knocking over her chair. With her arm, she made a wide swipe and knocked over the table next to the chair as well. The furniture thumping to the floor, the teapot shattering and the mayor's enraged shouts made a clamour that covered the sound of her footsteps as she dashed to the stairway door. Was it unlocked? She reached for the knob. Grunts and squeaks told her that the mayor was struggling to rise from his chair. She turned the knob and pulled, and the door sprang open. She closed the door behind her and leaped upward two steps at a time. Even in the pitch dark, she could climb stairs. In the room, the bell clanged and clanged, and the mayor bellowed.

When she got to the first landing, she heard the

guards shouting. There was a crash – someone must have fallen over the toppled chair or table. 'Where is she?' someone yelled. 'Must have run out the door!' Did they know which door? She didn't hear footsteps behind her.

If she could make it to the roof – and if from the roof she could jump to the roof of the Prison Room and from there to the street – then maybe she could escape. Her lungs were on fire now, her breath was burning her throat, but she climbed without stopping, and when she came to the top, she burst through the door to the roof and ran out.

And that was when the lights came back on. It was as if the blackout had been arranged especially for her. I am so lucky, she thought, so extremely lucky! Ahead of her was the clock tower. She went around to the other side of it. No dancing on the roof this time.

A low wall ran along the edge of the building. Lina approached it cautiously and peered out over the swarm of people assembling in Harken Square. Directly below her was the entrance of the Gathering Hall, and as she watched, two guards dashed out the door and down the steps. Good – they had gone the wrong way! They must think she'd escaped into the crowd. For the moment, she was safe. The clock in the tower began to chime. Three great booms rang out. It was time for the Singing to begin.

The Singing

Lina gazed down at the people of Ember, gathered to sing their songs. They stood so close together that she could see only their faces, which were lifted up towards the sky, with the hard bright lights shining down on them. They were silent, waiting for the Songmaster to appear on the Gathering Hall steps. There was a strange hush, as if the city were holding its breath. Of the whole Ember year, Lina thought, this hush before the Singing was one of the most exciting moments. She remembered other years, when she had stood with her parents, too short to see the Song-master's signal, too short to see anything but people's backs and legs, and waited for the first note to thunder out. She felt her heart move at that moment, every year. The sound would rise in waves around her like water, almost as if it could lift her off the ground.

Now suddenly the moment came again. From hundreds of voices rose the first notes of 'The Song of the City', deep and strong. She felt as she had all the years before: a quivering inside, as though a string under her ribs had been plucked, and a rush of joy and sadness mixed together. The deep, rumbling chords of the song filled Harken Square. Lina felt that she might step off the edge of the building and walk across the air, it seemed so solid with sound.

'The Song of the City' was long – there were verses about 'streets of light and walls of stone', about 'citizens with sturdy hearts', about 'stored abundance never-ending' (Not true, Lina thought). But at last, 'The Song of the City' wound down to its end. The singers held the final note, which grew softer and softer, and then there was silence again. Lina looked out at the lighted streets spreading away in every direction, the streets she knew so well. She loved her city, worn out and crumbling though it was. She looked up at the clock: ten minutes past three. Doon would be getting ready to leave for the Pipeworks. She didn't know whether he'd seen her being captured – if he had, he would be wondering if she'd been locked into the Prison Room. He'd be wondering if he should try to rescue her, or if he should go down the river by himself.

She should be hurrying to join him – but a sadness held her back, like a heavy stone in her chest. She bent her face into the palms of her hands and pressed hard against her closed eyes. How could she go away from Ember and leave Poppy behind? Because if she went, she must leave Poppy behind, mustn't she? How could she take her on a journey of such danger?

'The Song of the River' startled her when it began – the men's voices, low and rolling, swelling with power, and then the women's voices coming in above with a complicated melody that seemed to fight the current. Lina listened, unable to move. 'The Song of the River' made her uneasy – it always had. With its rolling, relentless rhythm, it seemed to urge her onward, saying, Go down, go away, go now. The more she listened, the more she felt something like the motion of the river in her stomach, a churning, sickening feeling.

Then came 'The Song of Darkness', the last of the three songs, and the one most filled with longing and majesty. The soul of Ember was in this song. Its tremendous chords held all the sorrow and all the strength of the people of the city. The song reached its climax: 'Darkness like an endless night,' sang the hundreds of voices, so powerfully the air seemed to shiver.

And at that moment, the lights once more went out. The voices faltered, but only for an instant. Then they rose again in the darkness, stronger even than before. Lina sang, too. She stood up and sang with all her might into the deep, solid blackness.

The last notes echoed and faded into a terrible silence. Lina stood utterly still. Will it end like this, she thought, at the finish of the last song? She felt the cold stone of the clock tower behind her back. She waited.

Then an idea came to her that made her skin prickle. What if she were to shout into the silence right now? What if she were to say, *Listen, people! We've found the way out of Ember! It's the river – we go on the river!* She could announce the astounding news, just as she and Doon had planned to do, and then – and then what would happen? Would the guards rush to the roof and seize her? Would the people in the square think her news was just a child's wishful thinking, or would they listen and be saved? She could feel the words pushing upwards in her throat, she wanted so much to say them. She took a deep breath and leaned forwards.

But before she could speak, a rumble of voices arose below. Someone shouted, 'Don't move!' and someone else shrieked. The rumble rose to a roar, and then cries flew into the darkness from everywhere. The crowd was erupting into panic.

There was no hope of being heard now. Lina clutched the edge of the clock tower as if the tumult below might cause her to fall. She strained her eyes against the darkness. Without light, she could go nowhere. Lights, come back on, she prayed. Come back on.

Then she saw something. At first, she thought her eyes were tricking her. She closed them tightly and opened them again. It was still there: a tiny point of light, moving. As she watched, it moved along slowly in a straight line. Then it turned and moved in a straight line again. Was it on River Road? She couldn't tell. But suddenly she knew what it was. It was Doon, with a candle. Doon, going towards the Pipeworks in the dark.

And she wanted to go, too. She could feel it all

through her, the urge to run and meet him and find the way out of Ember, to the new place. She listened to the shouts and wails of the terrified people in the square below. She thought of Mrs Murdo down there in the dark, being bumped and pushed, with her arms wrapped tightly around Poppy, trying to protect her, and all at once everything seemed clear. Lina knew what she would do – if only the lights would come back on, if only this was not the very last blackout in the history of Ember. Watching the tiny light following its steady course, she made a wish with the whole force of her heart and mind.

Then the floodlights flickered – there was a great cry of hope from the crowd – and the lights came on and stayed on. Lina ran to the back edge of the roof, dropped easily down onto the roof of the Prison Room and, seeing no guards in the crowd that was now streaming into the street, she jumped from there to the ground and joined the throng of people. She made her way down Greystone Street, going at the same pace as everyone else so she wouldn't stand out. When she came to the trash-can enclosure behind the Gathering Hall, she squatted down and hid. Her heart was beating fast, but she felt strong and purposeful now. She had her plan. As soon as she spotted Mrs Murdo and Poppy on their way home, she'd put it into action.

CHAPTER 17

Away

At three-twenty, Doon took his pillowcase pack, left the school by the back door, and started up Pibb Street. He went fast – the lights had gone out for a few minutes just before three, and he was nervous about being outside. He planned to take the long way to the Pipeworks, out at the very edge of the city, to avoid any guards that might still be looking for him.

He was filled with dread about Lina. He wouldn't know what had happened to her until he got to the Pipeworks and she either showed up or didn't. All he could do now was run.

He raced down Knack Street. It was strange to be out in the city with the streets so utterly deserted. Without the people passing back and forth, the streets seemed wider and darker. Nothing moved but himself, his shadow, and his fleeting reflection in shop windows he passed. In Selverton Square, he saw a kiosk where the poster with his and Lina's names on it had been pinned up. Everyone in the city must have seen these posters by now. He was famous, he thought wryly, but not in the way he'd wanted. There would be no glorious moment on the Gathering Hall steps after all. Instead of making his father proud, he would cause him dreadful worry.

This thought made him so sad that his knees felt suddenly wobbly. How could he just vanish without a word? But it was too late now, he couldn't go back. If only there was some way to send him a message – and in a moment, he realized there was. He stopped, fished in his pack for the paper and pencil he had brought, and scribbled on it, 'Father – We have found the way out – it was in the Pipeworks after all! You will know about it tomorrow. Love, Doon.' He folded this in quarters, wrote 'Deliver to Loris Harrow' in big letters on the outside and pinned it to the kiosk. There! That was the best he could do. He would have to trust that someone would deliver it.

In the distance, he heard the faint sound of singing. He listened – it was 'The Song of the River', just ending. *'Far below, like the blood of the earth, From the centre of nowhere rushing forth,'* he sang under his breath. Like everyone in Ember, he knew the words of the three songs by heart. He sang along softly with the faraway singers:

> *'Making the light for the lamps of Ember,*
> *Older than anyone can remember,*

Faster than anything anyone knows,
The river comes and the river goes.'

Up Rim Street now to River Road. He was halfway there. The singers were starting on 'The Song of Darkness'. It was his favourite, with its powerful, deep harmonies – he was a little sorry to be missing it. He went up the Pott Street side of empty Riverroad Square, where another poster hung crookedly on the kiosk, and he was headed towards North Street when suddenly the lights flickered and went out.

He jolted to a stop. Stand still and wait – that was his automatic response. In the distance he heard a dip in the sound of the singing, some startled voices breaking the flow, but then the song rose again, defying the darkness. For a moment all thoughts vanished from Doon's mind; there was nothing but the fearless words of the song:

'Black as sleep and deep as dreaming,
Darkness like an endless night.
Yet within the streets of Ember
Bright and bravely shines our light.'

He sang, standing still in the blackness. When the song ended, he waited. The lights would surely come back soon. For a few minutes there was silence, and then, far away but piercingly clear, he heard a scream.

More screams and shouts followed, the sounds of panic. He felt the panic himself, like a hand taking hold of him, making him want to leap up and fling himself against the dark.

But suddenly, with a flash of joy, he remembered: he didn't have to wait for the lights to come back on. He had what no citizen of Ember had ever had before – a way to see in the dark. He set his pack down, untied the knot at the top and groped around inside until he felt the candle. Down in a corner, he found the little packet of matches. He scraped a match against the pavement, and it flared up instantly. He held the flame to the string on the candle, and the string began to burn. He had a light. He had the only light in the entire city.

The candle didn't cast its light very far, but it was enough to see at least the pavement in front of him. He went slowly along Pott Street, then turned left on North Street. At the end of the street was the wall of the Pipeworks office.

When he got to the Pipeworks entrance, no one was there. A little cloud of moths came to flutter around the flame of his candle, but otherwise nothing moved in Plummer Square. There was nothing to do but wait. Doon blew the candle out – he didn't want to use it all up in case the lights stayed off a long time – and squatted down on the pavement, setting down his bundle and leaning against one of the big trash cans. He waited, listening to the distant shouts – and at last the lights blinked, blinked again and came on.

Lina was nowhere in sight. If the guards had found her and taken her . . . But Doon preferred not to think about that yet. He would wait for a while – she would have been delayed by the blackout if she was on her way. He couldn't see the clock tower from here, but it was probably not quite four o'clock.

What if she didn't come? The Singing was over, the people were dispersing throughout the city, and the guards, no doubt, would soon resume their search for him. Doon clasped his arms together and pressed them hard against his stomach, trying to stop the queasy fluttering.

If she didn't come, Doon had two choices: he could stay in the city and do what he could to save Lina, or he could go in the boat by himself and hope Lina could somehow free herself and tell the people of Ember about the way out. He didn't like either of these plans; he wanted to go down the river, and he wanted to go with Lina.

Doon stood up and hoisted his sack again. He was too restless to keep sitting. He walked down to Gappery Street and looked in both directions. Not a single person was in sight. He walked to Plummer Street, thinking that perhaps Lina was coming by way of the city's edge, as he had, to avoid being seen. But no one was there; he didn't even see anyone when he went past Subling Street to the very end of the city. He had to decide what to do.

He went and stood in the doorway of the Pipeworks. Think, he said to himself. Think! He was not even sure he *could* make the river journey by himself. How would he get the boat into the water? Could he lift it without help? On the other hand, how could he help Lina if she was in the hands of the mayor's guards? What could he possibly do that would not just get himself caught, too?

He felt sick. His hands were cold. He stepped out of the doorway and scanned the square once again. Nothing moved but the moths around the lights.

And then down Gappery Street Lina came running. She came across the square, and he dashed to meet her. She was hugging a bundle to her chest.

'I've come, I'm here, I almost didn't make it,' she said, breathing so hard she could barely talk. 'And look.' She folded back the blanket of her bundle. Doon saw a curl of brown hair and two wide frightened eyes. 'I've brought Poppy.'

Doon was so glad to see Lina that he didn't mind at all that Poppy was coming with them, making a risky journey even riskier. Relief and excitement flooded through him. They were going! They were going!

'OK,' he said. 'Come on!'

With his borrowed key, he opened the Pipeworks

door, and they hurried past the yellow slickers on their hooks and the lines of rubber boots. Doon dashed into the Pipeworks office long enough to replace the key on its hook, and then they pulled open the stairway door and started down. Lina stepped slowly because of Poppy, and Poppy clung to her neck, unusually quiet, sensing the strangeness and importance of what was happening. At the bottom of the stairs, they came out into the main tunnel and walked down the path to the west until they came to the marked rock.

'How are we going to get Poppy down there?' Doon asked.

Lina said, 'I'll fasten her to my chest.' Setting Poppy down, Lina took off the coat and the sweater she was wearing. With Doon's help, she made her sweater into a sling for Poppy, tying its sleeves behind her neck. Then she put her coat back on and buttoned it up.

Doon looked doubtfully at this bulky arrangement. 'Will you be able to climb down, carrying her like that? Will you be able to reach around her and hold onto the rungs?'

'Yes,' said Lina. Now that she had Poppy with her, she felt brave again. She could do whatever she needed to.

Doon went down first. Lina followed. 'Stay very still, Poppy,' she said. 'Don't squirm.' Poppy did stay still, but even so it was not easy going down the ladder with her extra weight. Lina's arms were just long enough to reach past Poppy and hold onto the ladder. She descended very slowly. When she got to the ledge, she stepped sideways, gripped the hand Doon held out for her and, with a deep breath of relief, came into the entryway.

They walked to the back of the entry hall, and Doon opened the steel panel and took out the key. He slid aside the door to the room where the single boat was, and they went in. Doon took his candle from his sack and lit it. Lina unwrapped Poppy and sat her down at the back of the room. 'Don't move from there,' she said. Poppy put her thumb in her mouth, and Doon and Lina set to work.

Doon's sack went in the pointed end of the boat, which they decided must be the front. They put the boxes of candles and matches into the rear of the boat. It was clear they'd been designed to go there; they fit snugly.

The poles labelled 'Paddles' were a mystery. Lina thought maybe they were weapons, meant for fending off hostile creatures. Doon thought they might fit across the boat somehow to make railings to brace yourself against, but he couldn't get them to work in this way. Finally, they decided just to leave the paddles in the bottom of the boat and figure out what they were for as they went along.

Doon dripped a bit of wax on the floor and stood his candle up in it, so he'd have both hands free. 'Let's see if we can lift the boat,' he said.

With Doon at the rear and Lina at the front, they found they could lift the boat with ease. It was amazingly light, even with the boxes and pack inside it. They set it down again. The next step was to get it in the water somehow, and then get in it themselves.

'We can't just drop it in,' Lina said. 'The river would grab it right away.'

'That must be what the ropes are for,' said Doon. 'We lower it in by holding onto the ropes. And tie the ropes to something to keep it from moving.'

'To what?'

'They must have put a peg or something in the wall to tie it to.' Doon went back out to the edge of the river and got down on his knees. Leaning over, he felt with one hand along the bank below. At first there was only smooth, slippery rock. He moved his hand slowly back and forth, up and down. River water splashed against his fingers. At last he felt something – a metal rod attached to the river wall, like the rungs of the ladder they had climbed down. 'I've found it,' he called.

He got up again and went back to the boat room. 'Let's carry the boat out,' he said. He and Lina lifted it and, taking small steps, moved it forward. As they went out the door, Poppy began to wail.

'Don't cry!' Lina called to her. 'Stay right there! We'll be back in a second.'

They carried the boat right to the edge of the water and set it down carefully, its front end pointing downstream. Doon knelt again, feeling for the metal rod. 'Hand me the end of the rope,' he said.

Which rope? Lina thought for a second. She realized it had to be the one attached to the side of the boat nearest her – that would be the side closest to the riverbank when they put the boat in. She uncoiled the rope, ran it around the boat, and handed its end down to Doon, who lay on his stomach with his head hanging over the edge and knotted the rope to the metal rung in the wall. He got to his feet again, wiping water from his face.

'Now,' Doon said, 'we can put the boat in the water.'

Another wail came from the boat room. 'I'm coming,' Lina called, and dashed back for Poppy. She hoisted her up and spoke into her ear, in the voice she used for announcing an exciting game: 'We're going on an *adventure*, Poppy. We're going for a *ride*, a ride in the water! It will be fun, sweetie, you'll see.' She blew out the candle Doon had left and carried Poppy to the river's edge.

'Are we ready?' said Doon.

'I guess we are.' Goodbye to Ember, Lina thought.

Goodbye to everyone, goodbye to everything. For a second, a picture of herself arriving in the bright city of her dreams flashed into her mind, and then it faded and was gone. She had no idea what lay ahead.

She set Poppy down against the wall of the entry passage. 'Sit here,' she told her. 'Don't move until I tell you to.' Poppy sat, her eyes wide, her plump legs sticking out in front of her.

Lina took hold of the rope at the rear of the boat. Doon took hold of the rope at the front. They heaved the boat up and stretched sideways to swing it out over the water. It tipped alarmingly from side to side. 'Let it down!' yelled Lina. They both let the ropes slide through their hands, and the boat fell and hit the water with a slap. It bounced and rocked and pulled against its tether, but Doon's knot held. The boat stayed in place, waiting for them.

'Here I go!' Doon cried. He bent over, gripped the rim of the boat with one hand, turned backwards, and stepped in. The boat tipped sideways under his weight. Doon staggered a step, and then found his balance. 'All right!' he yelled. 'Hand me Poppy!'

Lina lifted Poppy, who began to howl and kick at the sight of the bucking boat and the churning water. But Doon's arms were right there, and Lina thrust her into them. A second later, she jumped in herself, and then all three of them were tossed to the floor of the boat by its violent rocking.

Doon managed to get to his feet. He hauled on the rope that held the boat to the bank until he was close enough to reach the knot. He struggled with it. Water splashed into his face. He yanked at the knot, loosened it, pulled the rope free – and the boat shot forwards.

CHAPTER 18

Where the River Goes

For a second, Lina saw the banks of the river streak by. Ahead was the opening of the tunnel, like an enormous mouth. They plunged into it and left the light of the Pipeworks behind. In complete darkness, the boat pitched and rolled, and Lina, in the bottom of it, banged from side to side, gripping Poppy with one arm and grabbing with the other hand for anything to hold on to. Doon slid into her, and she slid into the boxes. Poppy was shrieking wildly.

'Doon!' Lina shouted, and he shouted back, 'Hold on! Hold on!' But she kept losing her grip on the edge of the boat and being flung sideways. She was terrified that Poppy would slam into the metal bench, or be torn from her arms and tossed into the river.

The boat hit something and shuddered, then raced on. It felt like being swallowed, this rushing through the dark, with the river roaring like a thousand voices.

Lina's legs were tangled with Doon's, and Poppy's

arms were so tight around her neck that she could hardly breathe. But it was the dark that was most terrible – going so fast into the dark.

She closed her eyes. If they were going to smash into a wall or plunge into a bottomless hole, there was nothing she could do about it. All she could do was hold tight to Poppy. She did that, for what seemed a long time.

And then at last the current slowed, and the boat stopped thrashing about so wildly. Lina managed to sit up, and she felt Doon moving, too. Poppy's shrieks turned to whimpers. The darkness was still complete, but Lina sensed space above and around her. Where were they? She had to *see*.

'Doon!' she said. 'Are you all right? Can you find us a candle?'

'I'll try,' Doon said. She felt him scramble past her to the back of the boat, and she heard a scrape as he pulled a box out from its place under the bench. 'Can't find the latch!' Doon said. Then a second later, 'There, I've got it. This is the matches, so this one must be candles.' More scraping and banging. The boat lurched, Lina slid forwards. Doon slid, too, and slammed into her back. He gave a yell of rage. 'Dropped the match! Hold on, I almost had it.' Long seconds of scrambling and clattering. Then a light flared up, and Doon's shadowed face appeared above it. He touched the match to a candle, and the light grew steadier.

It was only a small flame, but it cast glints of light on the tunnel walls and the silky surface of the water. The tunnel had an arched ceiling, Lina saw, like the tunnels of the Pipeworks, but it was much wider than those tunnels. The river ran through it like a moving road.

'Can you light another?' Lina asked. Doon nodded and turned back to the boxes, but once again the boat struck something, causing a spray of water to slap into them and put the candle out.

It was several minutes before Doon managed to light it again, and more before he finally had two burning at once. He jammed one of them into a space between the bench and the side of the boat, and he held the other in his hand. His hair was flattened against his forehead, and dripping. His brown jacket was torn at the shoulder. 'That's better,' he said.

It was better – not only did they have light to see by, but the current was slower, and the boat sailed more smoothly. Lina was able to unwrap Poppy from her neck and look around. Ahead she could see that the tunnel curved. The boat swung into the curve, banged against the wall, straightened itself and sped on. 'Hand me a candle, too,' she said.

Doon gave Lina the candle he was holding and lit another. They found places to wedge all three candles into the frame of the boat, so they could keep their hands free. For a while they rushed along almost silently, the river having become nearly as smooth as a sheet of glass.

Then suddenly the current slowed even more, and the tunnel opened out. 'We've come into a room,' said Lina. Far overhead arched a vaulted ceiling. Columns of rock hung down from it, and columns of rock rose from the water, too, making long shadows that turned and mingled as the boat floated among them. They glimmered in the candlelight, pink and pale green and silver. Their strange lumpy shapes looked like something soft that had frozen – like towers of mashed potatoes, Lina thought, that had hardened to stone.

Now and then the boat bumped into one of these columns, and they found that they could use a paddle to knock themselves free again. In this way they crossed the room to the other side, where again the passage narrowed and the current ran faster.

Much faster. It was as if the boat were being pulled forwards by a powerful hand. The water grew rough again, and splashes of spray put out their candles. Lina and Doon huddled in the bottom of the boat with Poppy between them, their arms clasped around her. They clenched their teeth and squeezed their eyes shut, and soon there was nothing in their minds but the roll and plunge of the boat and nothing in their bodies but the effort not to be thrown out.

Once, the sound of the river rose to a crashing, and the front of the boat tipped downwards, and they were pitched about so violently that it seemed they were tumbling down stairs – but that lasted only a few seconds, and then they were streaming onwards as before.

Lina lost track of time. But a while later, maybe a few minutes, maybe an hour, the current slowed. The candles they'd stuck in the boat had been knocked overboard, so Doon lit new ones. They saw that they had come to another pool. There were no lumpy columns of rock here; nothing interrupted the wide flat surface of the water, which stretched out before them in the flickering light from their candles. The ceiling was smooth and only about ten feet above their heads. The boat drifted, as if it had lost its sense of direction. Using a paddle to poke against the walls, Doon guided the boat around the edge of the pool.

'I don't see where the river goes on,' said Doon. 'Do you?'

'No,' said Lina. 'Unless it's there, where it flows into that little gap.' She pointed to a crack in the wall only a few inches wide.

'But the boat can't go there.'

'No, it's much too small.'

He poled the boat forwards. Their shadows moved with them along the wall.

'Wanna go home,' said Poppy.

'We're almost there,' Lina told her.

'We certainly can't go back the way we came,' said Doon.

'No.' Lina dipped a hand in the water. It was so cold it sent an ache up her arm.

'Could this be the end?' said Doon. His voice sounded flat in this closed-in place.

'The end?' Lina felt a shiver of fear.

'I mean the end of the trip,' Doon said. 'Maybe we're supposed to get out over there.' He pointed to a wide expanse of rock that sloped back into the darkness on one side of the pool. Everywhere else, the walls rose straight out of the water.

He poled the boat over to the rock slope. The boat scraped bottom here – the water was shallow. 'I'll get out and see if this goes anywhere,' said Lina. 'I want to be on solid ground again, anyway.' She handed Poppy to Doon and stood up. Holding a candle, she put one foot over the edge of the boat and into the cold water, and she waded ashore.

The way did not look promising. The ground sloped upwards, and the ceiling sloped downward. As she went farther back she had to stoop. A few yards in, a tumbled heap of rocks blocked the way. She inched around them, turning sideways to squeeze through the narrow space, and crept forwards, holding the candle out in front of her. This goes nowhere, she thought. We're trapped.

But a few steps farther along, she found she could stand up straight again, and a few steps beyond that she turned a corner, and suddenly the candlelight shone on a wide path, with a high ceiling and a smooth floor. Lina gave a wild shout. 'Here it is!' she cried. 'It's here! There's a path!'

Doon's voice came from far away. She couldn't tell what he was saying. She made her way back towards the boat, and when it came in sight she yelled again, 'I found a path! A path!'

Doon scrambled out and waded ashore, carrying Poppy. He set her down, and then he and Lina took hold of the boat and hauled it as far as they could up the slope of rock. Poppy caught the excitement. She shouted gleefully, waving her fists like little clubs, and stomped around, glad to be on her feet again. She found a pebble and plunked it into the water, crowing happily at the splash it made.

'I want to see the path,' said Doon.

'Go up that way,' Lina told him, 'and around the pile of rocks. I'll stay here and take things out of the boat.'

Doon went, taking another candle from the box in the boat. Lina sat Poppy down in a kind of nook formed by a roundish boulder and a hollow in the wall. 'Don't move from here,' she said. Then she pulled Doon's bundle from under the seat of the boat.

It was damp, but not soaked. Maybe the food inside would still be all right. She was hungry all of a sudden. She'd had no dinner, she remembered. It must be the middle of the night by now, or maybe even morning again.

She carried Doon's bundle ashore, along with the boxes of candles and matches, and as she set them down, Doon came back. His eyes were glowing, the reflection of a tiny flame dancing in each one. 'That's it for sure,' he said. 'We've made it.' Then his eyes shifted. 'What's Poppy got?' he asked.

Lina whipped around. In Poppy's hands was something dark and rectangular. It wasn't a stone. It was more like a packet of some kind. She was plucking and pulling at it. She lifted it to her mouth as if to tear it with her teeth – and Lina jumped to her feet. 'Stop!' she shouted. Poppy, startled, dropped the packet and began to cry.

'It's all right, never mind,' Lina said, retrieving what Poppy had been about to chew on. 'Come and have some dinner now. Hush, we're going to have dinner. I'm sure you're hungry.'

In the light of Doon's candle, with Poppy squirming on Lina's lap, they examined Poppy's find. The packet was wrapped in slippery, greenish material and bound up with a strap. It wasn't wrapped very well; it looked as if someone had bundled it up quickly. The material was loose, and blotched with whitish mould.

Lina edged the strap off carefully. It was partly rotten; on the end of it was a small square buckle, covered with rust. She folded back the wrapping.

Doon took a sharp breath. 'It's a book,' he said. He moved his candle closer, and Lina opened the brown cover. The pages inside had faint blue lines across them, and someone had written along these lines in slanted black letters, which were not neat like the writing in the library books, but sprawling, as if the writer had been in a hurry.

Doon ran his finger under the first line. 'It says, *They tell us we* . . . learn? . . . No, leave. *They tell us we leave tonight.*'

He looked up and met Lina's eyes.

'Leave?' said Lina. 'From where?'

'From Ember?' Doon asked. 'Could someone have come this way before us?'

'Or was it someone leaving the other city?'

Doon looked down at the book again. He rifled through the pages – there were many of them.

'Let's save it,' said Lina. 'We'll read it when we get to the new city.'

Doon nodded. 'It'll be easier to see there.'

So Lina wrapped up the book again and tied it securely into Doon's bundle. They sat on the rock shelf for a while, eating the food Doon had brought. The candles wedged in the boat still shone steadily, and their light was cosy, like lamplight. It made golden shapes on the still surface of the pond.

Doon said, 'I saw the guards run after you. Tell me what happened.'

Lina told him.

'And what about Poppy? What did you tell Mrs Murdo?'

'I told her the truth – at least I hope it's the truth. I caught up with her on her way home after the Singing. She'd seen the posters – she was terrified – but before she could ask questions, I just said she must give Poppy to me. I said I was taking her to safety. Because that's what I suddenly realized on the roof of the Gathering Hall, Doon. I'd been thinking before that I *had* to leave Poppy because she'd be safe with Mrs Murdo. But when the lights went out, I suddenly knew: there *is* no safety in Ember. Not for long. Not for anyone. I couldn't leave her behind. Whatever happens to us now, it's better than what's going to happen there.'

'And did you explain all that to Mrs Murdo?'

'No. I was in a terrible hurry to get to the Pipeworks and meet you, and I knew I had to go while there were still crowds in the street, so it would be harder for the guards to see me. I just said I was taking Poppy to safety. Mrs Murdo handed her over, but she sort of sputtered, "Where?" and "Why?" And I said, "You'll know in a few days – it's all right." And then I ran.'

'So you gave her the note, then?' said Doon. 'The one meant for Clary?'

'Oh!' Lina stared at him, stricken. 'The message to Clary!' She put her hand in her pocket and pulled out the crumpled piece of paper. 'I forgot all about it! All I was thinking of was getting Poppy and getting to you.'

'So no one knows about the room full of boats.'

Lina just shook her head, her eyes wide. 'How will we get back to tell them?'

'We can't.'

'Doon,' said Lina, 'if we'd told people right away, even just a few people . . . if we hadn't decided to be grand and announce it at the Singing . . .'

'I know,' said Doon. 'But we didn't, that's all. We didn't tell, and now no one knows. I did leave a message for my father, though.' He told Lina about pinning his last-minute message to the kiosk in Selverton Square. 'I said we'd found the way out, and that it was in the Pipeworks. But that's not much help.'

'Clary has seen the Instructions,' Lina said. 'She knows there's an egress. She might find it.'

'Or she might not.'

There was nothing to be done about it, and so they put the supplies back into Doon's pillowcase and got ready to go. Lina used Doon's rope to make a leash for Poppy. She tied one end around Poppy's waist and the other around her own. She filled her pockets with packs of matches, and Doon put all the remaining candles in his sack – in case they arrived in the new city at night. He filled his bottle with river water, lit a candle for himself and one for Lina, and thus equipped, they left the boat behind and crept up the rocky shelf to the path.

CHAPTER 19

A World of Light

As they squeezed past the rocks at the entrance to the path, Doon thought he saw the candlelight glance off a shiny place on the wall. He stopped to look, and when he saw what it was, he called out to Lina, who was a few steps ahead of him. 'There's a notice!'

It was a framed sign, bolted to the stone, a printed sheet behind a piece of glass. Dampness had seeped under the glass and made splotches on the paper, but by holding their candles up close, they could read it.

Welcome, Refugees from Ember!
This is the final stage of your journey.
Be prepared for a climb
that will take several hours.
Fill your bottles with water from the river.
We wish you good fortune,
The Builders

'They're expecting us!' said Lina.

'Well, they wrote this a long time ago,' Doon said. 'The people who put it here must all be dead by now.'

'That's true. But they wished us good fortune. It makes me feel as if they're watching over us.'

'Yes. And maybe their great-great-great-grand-children will be there to welcome us.'

Encouraged, they started up the path. Their candles made only a feeble glow, but they could tell that the path was quite wide. The ceiling was high over their heads. The path seemed to have been made for a great company of people. In some places, the ground beneath their feet was rutted in parallel grooves, as if a wheeled cart of some kind had been driven over it. After they had walked a while, they realized that they were moving in long zigzags. The path would go in one direction for some time and then turn sharply and go the opposite way.

As they went along, they talked less and less; the path sloped relentlessly upwards, and they needed their breath just for breathing. The only sound was the light *pat-pat* of their footsteps. Lina and Doon took turns carrying Poppy on their backs – she had got tired of walking very soon and cried to be picked up. Twice, they stopped and sat down to rest, leaning against the walls of the passage and taking drinks from Doon's bottle of water.

'How many hours do you think we've been

walking?' Lina asked.

'I don't know,' Doon said. 'Maybe two. Maybe three. We must be nearly there.'

They climbed on and on. Their first candles had long ago burned down to the last inch, as had their second candles. Finally, when their third ones were about halfway gone, Lina began to notice that the air smelled different. The cold, sharp-edged, rock smell of the tunnel was changing to something softer, a strange, lovely smell. As they rounded a corner, a gust of this soft air swept past them, and their candles went out.

Doon said, 'I'll find a match,' but Lina said, 'No, wait. Look.'

They were not in complete darkness. A faint haze of light shone in the passage ahead of them. 'It's the lights of the city,' breathed Lina.

Lina set Poppy down. 'Quick, Poppy,' she said, and Poppy began to trot, keeping close at Lina's heels. The strange, lovely smell in the air grew stronger. The passage came to an end a few yards farther along, and before them was an opening like a great empty doorway. Without a word, Lina and Doon took hold of each other's hands, and Lina took hold of Poppy's. When they stood in the doorway and looked out, they saw no new city at all, but something infinitely stranger: a land vast and spacious beyond any of their dreams, filled with air that seemed to move, and lit by a shining silver circle hanging in an immense black sky.

In front of their feet, the ground swept away in a long, gentle slope. It was not bare stone, as in Ember; something soft covered it, like silvery hair, as high as their knees. Down the slope was a tumble of dark, rounded shapes, and then another slope rose beyond that. Way off into the distance, as far as they could see, the land lay in rolling swells, with clumps of shadow in the low places between them.

'Doon!' cried Lina. 'More lights!' She pointed at the sky.

He looked up and saw them – hundreds and hundreds of tiny flecks of light, strewn like spilled salt across the blackness. 'Oh!' he whispered. There was nothing else to say. The beauty of these lights made his breath stop in his throat.

They took a few steps forward. Doon bent to feel the strands that grew out of the ground, almost higher than Poppy's head; they were cool and smooth and soft, and there was dampness on them.

'Breathe,' said Lina. She opened her mouth and took in a long breath of air. Doon did the same.

'It's sweet,' he said. 'So full of smells.'

They held their hands out to feel the long stems as they waded slowly through them. The air moved against their faces and in their hair.

'Hear those sounds?' said Doon. A high, thin chirruping sound came from somewhere nearby. It was repeated over and over, like a question.

'Yes,' said Lina. 'What could it be?'

'Something alive, I think. Maybe some kind of bug.'

'A bug that sings.' Lina turned to Doon. Her face was shadowy in the silver light. 'It's so strange here, Doon, and so huge. But I'm not afraid.'

'No. I'm not either. It feels like a dream.'

'A dream, yes. Maybe that's why it feels familiar. I might have dreamed about this place.'

They walked until they came to where the dark shapes billowed up from the ground. These were plants, they discovered, taller than they were, with stems as hard and thick as the walls of houses, and leaves that spread out over their heads. On the slope beside these plants, they sat down.

'Do you think there is a city here somewhere?' Lina asked. 'Or any people at all?'

'I don't see any lights,' Doon said, 'even far off.'

'But with this silver lamp in the sky, maybe they don't need lights.'

Doon shook his head doubtfully. 'People would need more light than this,' he said. 'How could you see well enough to work? How could you grow your food? It's a beautiful light, but not bright enough to live by.'

'Then what shall we do, if there's no city, and no people?'

'I don't know. I don't know.' Doon didn't feel like thinking. He was tired of figuring things out. He wanted to look at this new world, and take in the scent of it and the feel of it, and figure things out later.

Lina felt the same way. She stopped asking questions, drew Poppy onto her lap, and gazed in silence at the glimmering landscape. After a while, she became aware that something strange was happening. Surely, when she had first sat down, the silver circle was just above the highest branch of the tall plant. Now the branch cut across it. As she watched, the circle sank very slowly down, until it was hidden, except for a gleam of brightness, behind the leaves.

'It's moving,' she said to Doon.

'Yes.'

A little later, it seemed to her that her eyes were blurring. There was a fuzziness in the sky, especially around the edges. It took a while for her to realize what was making the fuzziness.

'Light,' she said.

'I see it,' said Doon. 'It's getting brighter.'

The edge of the sky turned grey, and then pale orange, and then deep fiery crimson. The land stood out against it, a long black rolling line. One spot along this line grew so bright they could hardly look at it, so bright it seemed to take a bite out of the land. It rose higher and higher until they could see that it was a fiery circle, first deep orange and then yellow, and too bright to look at any longer. The colour seeped out of the sky and washed over the land. Light sparkled on the soft hair of the hills and shone through the lacy leaves as every shade of green sprang to life around them.

They lifted their faces to the astonishing warmth. The sky arched over them, higher than they could have imagined, a pale, clear blue. Lina felt as though a lid that had been on her all her life had been lifted off. Light and air rushed through her, making a song, like the songs of Ember, only it was a song of joy. She looked at Doon, and saw that he was smiling and crying at the same time, and she realized that she was, too.

Everything around them was springing to life. A glorious racket came from the branches – tweedling notes, peeps, burbles, high sharp calls. Bugs? wondered Doon, imagining with awe the bugs that could make such sounds. But then he saw something fly from a cluster of leaves and swoop down low across the ground, making a clear, sweet call as it flew. 'Did you see that?' he said to Lina, pointing. 'And there's another one! And there!'

'There there there there!' repeated Poppy, leaping from Lina's lap and whirling around, pointing in every direction.

The air was full of them now. They were much too large to be insects. One of them lit nearby on a stem. It looked at them with two bright black eyes and, opening its mouth, which was pointed like a thorn, sent forth a little trill.

'It's speaking to us,' said Doon. 'What could it be?'

Lina just shook her head. The little creature shifted its clawlike feet on the stem, flapped its brown wings, and trilled again. Then it leapt into the air and was gone.

They leapt up, too, and threw themselves into exploration. The ground was alive with insects – so many that Doon just laughed in helpless wonder. Flowers bloomed among the green blades, and a stream ran at the foot of the hill. They roamed over the green-coated slopes, running, sliding, calling out to each other with each new discovery, until they were exhausted. Then they sat down by the entrance to the path to eat what was left of their food. They untied Doon's bundle, and Lina suddenly cried out. 'The book! We forgot about the book!'

There it was, wrapped in its blotched green cloth.

'Let's read it out loud while we eat,' said Doon.

Lina opened the fragile notebook and laid it on the ground in front of her. She picked up a carrot with one hand, and with the other she kept her place on the scribbled page. This is what she read.

CHAPTER 20

The Last Message

Friday

They tell us we leave tonight. I knew it would be soon – the training has been over for nearly a month now – but still it feels sudden, it feels like a shock. Why did I agree to do this? I am an old woman, too tired to take up a new life. I wish now that I'd said no when they asked me.

I have put everything I can into my one suitcase – clothes, shoes, a good wind-up clock, some soap, an extra pair of glasses. Bring no books, they said, and no photographs. We have been told to say nothing, ever again, about the world we come from. But I am going to take this notebook anyhow. I am determined to write down what happens. Someday, someone may need to know.

Saturday

I went to the train station yesterday

evening, as they told me to, and got on the train they told me to take. It took us through Spring Valley, and I gazed out the window at the fields and houses of the place I was saying goodbye to – my home, and my family's home for generations. I rode for two hours, until the train reached a station in the hills. When I arrived, they met me – three men in suits – and drove me to a large building, where they led me down a corridor and into a big room full of other people – all with suitcases, most with grey or white hair. Here we have been waiting now for more than an hour.

They have spent years and years making this plan. It's supposed to ensure that, no matter what happens, people won't disappear from the earth. Some say that will never happen anyhow. I'm not so sure. Disaster seems very close. Everything will be all right, they tell us, but only a few people believe them. Why, if it's going to be all right, do we see it getting worse every day?

And of course this plan is proof that they think the world is doomed. All the best scientists and engineers have been pulled in to work on it. Extraordinary efforts have been made – efforts that would have done more good elsewhere. I think it's the wrong answer. But they asked me if I would go – I suppose because I've spent my life on a farm and I know about growing food. In spite of my doubts, I said yes. I'm not sure why.

There are a hundred of us, fifty men and fifty women. We are all at least sixty years old. There will be a hundred babies, too – two babies for each pair of 'parents'. I don't know yet which one of these gentlemen I'll be matched with. We are all strangers to one another. They planned it that way; they said there would be fewer memories between us. They want us to forget everything about the lives we've led and the places we've lived. The babies must grow up with no knowledge of a world outside, so that they feel no sorrow for what they have lost.

I hear some noises across the room. I think it's the babies arriving . . . Yes, here they come, each being carried by one of those grey-suited men. So many of them! So small! Little scrunched-up faces, tiny fists waving. I must stop for now. They're going to pass them out.

Later
We're travelling again, on a bus this time. It is night, I think, though it's hard to be sure because they have boarded up the windows of

the bus from the outside. They don't want us to know where we're going.

I have a baby on my lap – a girl. She has a bright pink face and no hair at all. Stanley, who sits next to me, holds a boy baby, with brown skin and a few tufts of black hair. Stanley and I are the keepers of these children. Our task is to raise them in this new place we're going to. By the time they are twenty or so, we'll be gone. They'll be on their own, making a new world.

Stanley and I have named these children Star and Forest.

Sunday

The buses have stopped, but they have not allowed us to get out yet. I can hear crickets singing, and smell the grass, so we must be in the country, and it must be night. I am very tired.

What kind of place can this be, safe from earthly catastrophes? All I can guess is that it must be underground. The thought fills me with dread. I'll try to sleep a little now.

Later

There was no chance to sleep. They called us off the buses, and we stepped out into a landscape of rolling hills, in full moonlight. 'That's the way we'll be going in,' they told us, pointing to a dark opening in the hill we stood on. 'Form a line there, please.' We did so. It was very quiet, except for the squalling of a few of the babies. If the others were like me, they were saying goodbye to the world. I reached down to touch the grass and breathed deeply to smell the earth. My eyes swept over the silver hills, and I thought of the animals prowling softly in the shadows or sleeping in their burrows, and the birds standing beneath the leaves of the trees, with their heads tucked under their wings. Last, I raised my eyes to the moon, which smiled down on us from a long, cold distance away. The moon will still be here when they come out, I thought. The moon and the hills, at least.

The opening led us into a winding passage that ran steeply downhill for perhaps a mile. It was hard going for me; my legs are not strong any more. We moved very slowly. The last part was the worst: a rocky slope where it was easy to miss your footing and slip. This led down to a pool. By the shore of the pool our group of aged pioneers gathered. Motorboats were waiting here for us, equipped with lanterns.

'When it's time for people to leave this

*place, is this the way they will come?' I asked
our pilot, who has a kind face. He said yes.*

*'But how will they know there's a way out,
if no one tells them?' I said. 'How will they
know what to do?'*

*'They're going to have instructions,' said
the pilot. 'They won't be able to get at the
instructions until the time is right. But when
they need them, the instructions will be there.'*

*'But what if they don't find them? What if
they never come out again?'*

*'I think they will. People find a way
through just about anything.'*

*That was all he would say. I am writing
these notes while our pilot loads the boat. I
hope he doesn't notice.*

'It ends there,' said Lina, looking up.

'He must have noticed,' said Doon. 'Or she was
afraid he would, so she decided to hide it instead of
taking it with her.'

'She must have hoped someone would find it.'

'Just as we did.' He pondered. 'But we might not
have, if it hadn't been for Poppy.'

'No. And we wouldn't have known that we came
from here.'

The fiery circle had moved up in the sky now, and
the air was so warm that they took off their coats.

Absently, Doon dug his finger into the ground, which was soft and crumbly. 'But what was the disaster that happened in this place?' he said. 'It doesn't look ruined to me.'

'It must have happened a long, long time ago,' said Lina. 'I wonder if people still live here.'

They sat looking out over the hills, thinking of the woman who had written in the notebook. What had her city been like? Lina wondered. Like Ember in some way, she imagined. A city with trouble, where people argued over solutions. A dying city. But it was hard to picture a city like Ember here in this bright, beautiful place. How could anyone have allowed such a place to be harmed?

'What do we do now?' asked Lina. She wrapped the notebook in its covering again and set it aside. 'We can't go back up the river and tell them all to come here.'

'No. We could never make the boat go against that current.'

'Are we here alone, then, for ever?'

'Maybe there's another way in, some way that lets you walk down to Ember. Or maybe there's another river that runs the other way. We have candles now, we could cross the Unknown Regions if we found a way to get there.'

This was the only plan they could come up with. So, all day long, they searched for another way in.

The Last Message

Under the brow of the hill, they found a hole where a stream wandered into the dark. The water was good to drink, but the hole was far too small for them to through. There were gullies full of shrubs, and Lina and Doon crawled among the leaves and prickly branches, but found no openings. Bugs buzzed around their ankles and past their eyes; brown earth stained their hands, and pebbles got into their shoes. Their thick, dark, shabby clothes got all full of prickly things, and since they were much too hot anyhow, they took most of them off. They had never felt such warmth against their skin and such soft air.

When the bright circle was at the top of the sky, they sat for a while in the shade of one of the tall plants on the side of the hill, in a place where the thick brush gave way to a clearing. Poppy went to sleep, but Lina and Doon sat looking out over the land. Green was everywhere, in different shades, like a huge, brilliant, gorgeous version of the overlapping carpets back in the rooms of Ember. Far away, Lina saw a narrow grey line curving like a pencil stroke across a sweep of green. She pointed this out to Doon, and both of them squinted hard at it, but it was too far away to see clearly.

'Could it be a road?' said Lina.

'It could,' said Doon.

'Maybe there are people here after all.'

'I hope so,' said Doon. 'There's so much I want to know.'

They were still gazing at the far-off bit of grey when they heard something moving in the brush nearby. Leaves rustled. There was a scraping, shuffling sound. They stiffened and held their breath. The shuffling paused, then started up again. Was it a person? Should they call out? But before they could decide what to do, a creature stepped into the clearing.

It was about the same size as Poppy, only lower to the ground, because it walked on four legs instead of two. Its fur was a deep rust-red. Its face was a long triangle, its ears stood up in points, and its black eyes shone. It trotted forwards a few steps, absorbed in its own business. Behind it floated a thick, soft-looking tail.

All at once it saw them and stopped.

Lina and Doon stayed absolutely still. So did the creature. Then it took a step towards them, paused, tilted its head a little as if to get a better look, and took another step. They could see the sheen of its fur and the glint of light in its eyes.

For a long moment, they stayed like this, frozen, staring at one another. Then, unhurriedly, the creature moved away. It pushed its nose among the leaves on the ground, wandering back towards the bushes, and when it raised its head again, they saw that it was holding something in its white teeth, something round and purplish. With a last glance at them, it leaped towards the bushes, its tail sailing, and disappeared.

Lina let out her breath and turned to look at Doon, whose mouth was open in astonishment. His voice shaky, he said, 'That was the most wonderful thing I have ever seen, ever in my whole life.'

'Yes.'

'And it saw us,' Doon said, and Lina nodded. They both felt it – they had been seen. The creature was utterly strange, not like anything they had ever known, and yet when it looked at them, some kind of recognition passed between them. 'I know now,' said Doon. 'This is the world we belong in.'

A few minutes later, Poppy woke up and made fretful noises, and Lina gave her the last of the peas in Doon's pack. 'What was that, do you think, in the creature's mouth?' she asked. 'Would it be something we could eat, a fruit of some kind? It looked like the pictures of peaches on cans, except for the colour.'

They got up and poked around, and soon they came across a plant whose branches were laden with the purple fruits, about the size of small beets, only softer. Doon picked one and cut it open with his knife. There was a stone inside. Red juice ran out over his hands. Cautiously, he touched his tongue to it.

'Sweet,' he said.

'If the creature can eat it, maybe we can, too,' said Lina. 'Shall we?'

They did. Nothing had ever tasted better. Lina cut the stones out and gave chunks of the fruit to Poppy. Juice ran down their chins. When they had eaten five or six apiece, they licked their sticky fingers clean and started to explore again.

They went higher up the slope they were on, wading through flowers as high as their waists, and near the top they came upon a kind of dent in the ground, as if a bit of the earth had caved in. They walked down into it, and at the end of the dent they found a crack about as tall as a person but not nearly as wide as a door. Lina edged through it sideways and discovered a narrow tunnel. 'Send Poppy through,' she called back to Doon, 'and come yourself.' But it was dark inside, and Doon had to go back to where he'd left his pack to get a candle. By candlelight, they crept along until they came to a place where the tunnel ended abruptly. But it ended not with a wall but with a sudden huge nothingness that made them gasp and step back. A few feet beyond their shoes was a sheer, dizzying drop. They looked out into a cave so enormous that it seemed almost as big as the world outside. Far down at the bottom shone a cluster of lights.

'It's Ember,' Lina whispered.

They could see the tiny bright streets crossing each other, and the squares, little chips of light, and the dark tops of buildings. Just beyond the edges was the immense darkness.

'Oh, our city, Doon. Our city is at the bottom of a hole!' She gazed down through the gulf, and all of what she had believed about the world began to slowly break apart. '*We* were underground,' she said. 'Not just the Pipeworks. Everything!' She could hardly make sense of what she was saying.

Doon crouched on his hands and knees, looking over the edge. He squinted, trying to see minute specks that might be people. 'What's happening there, I wonder?'

'Could they hear us if we shouted?'

'I don't think so. We're much too far up.'

'Maybe if they looked into the sky they'd see our candle,' said Lina. 'But no, I guess they wouldn't. The streetlamps would be too bright.'

'Somehow, we have to get word to them,' said Doon, and that was when the idea came to Lina.

'Our message!' she cried. 'We could send our message!'

And they did. From her pocket, Lina took the message that Doon had written, the one that was supposed to have gone to Clary, explaining everything. In small writing, they squeezed in this note at the top:

Dear People of Ember,

   We came down the river from the Pipeworks and
found the way to another place. It is green here and
very big. Light comes from the sky. You must follow the
instructions in this message and come on the river.
Bring food with you. Come as quickly as you can.
                    Lina Mayfleet and Doon Harrow

They wrapped the message in Doon's shirt and put a rock inside it. Then they stood in a row at the edge of the chasm, Doon in the middle holding Poppy's hand and Lina's. Lina took aim at the heart of the city, far beneath her feet. With all her strength, she cast the message into the darkness, and they watched as it plunged down and down.

Mrs Murdo, walking even more briskly than usual to keep her spirits up, was crossing Harken Square when something fell to the pavement just in front of her with a terrific thump. How extraordinary, she thought, bending to pick it up. It was a sort of bundle. She began to untie it.

ACKNOWLEDGEMENTS

My thanks to the friends who read and and commented helpfully on my manuscript: Susie Mader, Patrick Daly, Andrew Ramer, Charlotte Muse, Sara Jenkins, Mary Dederer and Pat Carr. My gratitude to my agent, Nancy Gallt, who brought *The City of Ember* into the light, and my editor, Jim Thomas, who made it the best book it could be. And my love and thanks to my mother, my first and best writing teacher.

THE ADVENTURE CONTINUES . . .

THE PEOPLE OF SPARKS
by Jeanne DuPrau

The exciting sequel to
The City of Ember

Lina and Doon led the citizens of Ember to safety,
to a new and frightening world full of colour and life.
They have nothing, but the people of Sparks do seem
to want to help them – at least at first . . .

But as differences between the two groups grow
into resentment, hatred and violence, the two teenagers
must find a way to bring the people of Ember and
Sparks together – before they face disaster again . . .

ISBN: 978 0 552 55239 4

NOW A MAJOR MOTION PICTURE!

The *Sunday Times* Bestseller

ERAGON

By Christopher Paolini

*WHAT WAS ONCE YOUR LIFE
IS NOW YOUR LEGEND*

When Eragon finds a polished blue stone in the forest, he thinks it is the lucky discovery of a poor farm boy. But when the stone brings a dragon hatchling, Eragon soon realizes he has stumbled upon a legacy nearly as old as the Empire itself.

Overnight he is thrust into a perilous new world of destiny, magic, and power. With only an ancient sword and the advice of an old storyteller for guidance, Eragon and the fledgling dragon must navigate the dangerous terrain and dark enemies of an Empire ruled by a king whose evil knows no bounds.

Can Eragon take up the mantle of the legendary Dragon Riders? The fate of the Empire may rest in his hands.

ISBN: 978 0 552 55371 1

The first action-packed adventure in a new
blockbuster series from James Patterson, the
world's bestselling thriller writer.

THE DANGEROUS
DAYS OF DANIEL X

by James Patterson

*"The aliens are here," I whispered,
and reached up and clicked off the
basement light. I prepared to be
eaten, or maybe worse . . .*

Fifteen-year-old alien hunter Daniel X is on a
mission to finish the job that killed his parents – to
wipe out the world's most bloodthirsty aliens on The
List. At the number-one spot, The Prayer is Daniel's
ultimate target. With mind-blowing skills like telepathy
and the ability to transform and create, Daniel's
got more than a few tricks up his sleeve.

But for now there are plenty of gruesome enemies
in the way as along with his friends, Daniel hunts
down the aliens on The List – one by one. But as he
battles towards his top target he can't forget one thing:
he's got a host of aliens to fight, but on their lists
there's only one name at the top . . . and that's his.

ISBN: 978 0 385 61376 7

**A breathtaking new adventure series from
the real-life survival expert,
BEAR GRYLLS**

MISSION SURVIVAL:
GOLD OF THE GODS

by Bear Grylls

Beck Granger is facing certain death. He's lost
in the Colombian jungle, with no GPS, no food,
and no help but for two friends, with only a tattered
map and a strange amulet guiding their way.
But he has his survival skills – and if anyone
can keep them alive, Beck can.

Building rafts and shelter . . .
Killing snakes . . .
Finding water . . .
Fending off shark attacks . . .

He knows how to navigate any environment – but
even he can't anticipate every danger . . .

Hot on the trail of his kidnapped uncle, Beck must
race against time and the elements. Can he find the lost
City of Gold and discover the secret of its people?

ISBN: 978 1 862 30479 6

A MAGICAL ADVENTURE FROM BESTSELLING AUTHORS STEVE COLE AND LINDA CHAPMAN

GENIE US!

By Steve Cole and Linda Chapman

What would you wish for . . . ?

Take four ordinary children . . .
A genie in the shape of
a bookworm . . .
And a magical book.

Then get ready for more adventure
and mayhem then you could ever imagine!

Join Michael, Milly, Jason and Jess as they dive into
a world of weirdness and wonder, trouble and trickery,
trying to make each other's wishes come true.

But when their wishes start to go wrong,
the magic seems scarier. If the children's greatest
wish of all is finally granted, will their world
change for better or for worse?

ISBN: 978 1 862 30343 0